Celebrate the Season

Home for the Holidays

Celebrate the Season

Home for the Holidays

by
Taylor Garland

Little, Brown and Company
New York Boston

Copyright © 2018 by Hachette Book Group

Jacket art © Ermolaev Alexander/Shutterstock.com (cats), Didecs/Shutterstock.com (ribbon), digieye/Shutterstock.com (bow/frame), © olegganko/Shutterstock.com (snowflake background) Snowflakes © Stock Vector One/Shutterstock.com Cover design by Cassie Gonzales Cover © 2018 Hachette Book Group, Inc.

Little, Brown and Company
Hachette Book Group
1290 Avenue of the Americas, New York, NY 10104
Visit us at LBYR.com

First Edition: October 2018

Little, Brown and Company is a division of Hachette Book Group, Inc. The Little, Brown name and logo are trademarks of Hachette Book Group, Inc.

The publisher is not responsible for websites (or their content) that are not owned by the publisher.

Library of Congress Control Number: 2018942285

ISBNs: 978-0-316-41299-5 (pbk), 978-0-316-41298-8 (ebook)

Printed in the United States of America

LSC-C

Paperback: 10 9 8 7 6 5 4 3 2 1

Chapter 1

"Do you want some OJ, Cody?" Alyssa Sing called to her brother from the kitchen.

"Nah," came his muffled reply a moment later.

Alyssa took a glass down from the cupboard and poured herself some juice. Then, just as she was placing the carton back in the refrigerator, her brother's voice rang out again.

"Actually, yeah, I'll take some juice."

Alyssa sighed good-naturedly and poured her brother a glass of juice. After placing the carton back in the refrigerator, she walked into the den, handed

Cody his juice, and settled down on the couch next to him. Cody grunted.

"And what do you say when someone does something nice for you?" Alyssa prompted.

Cody pretended to be deep in thought. "Well, when someone does something nice for me, I give my heartfelt thanks."

Alyssa nodded. "And..."

"And all you did was pour me some juice," Cody concluded. "I hardly think that warrants heartfelt thanks."

"You're hopeless," Alyssa told him, taking a sip of her juice. She tried fixing him with an angry stare but couldn't quite pull it off, especially not after Cody did a hilarious impression of her fake angry face. Alyssa laughed so hard she almost spit her juice out.

"Ugh, if that's what I look like, remind me never to make that face," she said between giggles.

"You wish you looked this good," Cody replied, twisting his face into an even sillier expression.

Alyssa and Cody were only a year apart, Alyssa in seventh grade and Cody in eighth. Alyssa thought about how, when they were younger, they were often mistaken for twins. In the past year or two, though, Cody had grown a lot and was now a good five inches taller than his sister. No one really mistook them for twins anymore. Alyssa thought that the height difference could be why, but their vastly different personalities also had a lot to do with it. Cody was confident and outgoing and Alyssa was...shy. She wasn't shy at home with her mom and brother, but that was because she was so comfortable with them. Cody seemed to attract friends like a magnet, but Alyssa was struggling a little in that department lately. It wasn't that Alyssa didn't want to make friends. She really did. In fact, she *loved* making friends. It was just really hard to do sometimes. Especially after moving to a new town and starting at a new school like they had just a few months ago.

Alyssa's thoughts were interrupted by the sound of the kitchen door opening.

"Hey, kids," Melanie Sing called from the kitchen. She sounded a little breathless.

"How was your run, Mom?" Alyssa asked.

Mrs. Sing strode into the living room and plopped down on the recliner. "It was good, thanks. It's gorgeous outside—must be close to seventy already! Let's open up some windows."

Alyssa got up from the couch and walked over to the nearest window on one side of the room while her brother tackled the windows on the other side. She carefully unlatched the lock and then pulled open the window. Immediately, she was greeted with a warm burst of air.

"December eighth and it's seventy degrees outside," Alyssa said. "I'm not sure I will ever get used to this."

The Sing family had moved to Palm Meadows, Florida, from Massachusetts in August. In addition to having a whole new town and school to get used to, there was also a new climate for Alyssa to adjust to. One where it was warm all year round.

"What's to get used to?" Cody asked as he settled back on the couch. "The weather here is perfect for soccer all year long. End of story."

"There's more to life than soccer," Alyssa replied.

"Like—" She held up her hand to shush her brother just as he was about to ask *Like what?*

"Like...white Christmases, for example," Alyssa said finally. "Does it really not bug you at all that we will probably be wearing shorts on Christmas Day?"

"Nope, not one bit," Cody said.

Just then his phone rang and he ran to answer it from the privacy of his room.

"I know a warm-weather Christmas takes some getting used to," Mrs. Sing spoke from the recliner as she tugged off her sneakers. "But we will still make this Christmas really special."

"Oh, I know," Alyssa said quickly. She immediately felt guilty. Had she made her mom feel bad? "I'm sorry I complained, Mom. I like it here. And I know Christmas will still be great!"

Her mom got up from the recliner and sat down next to Alyssa on the sofa. "Sweetie, it's okay to be a little bummed about not having a white Christmas. It doesn't hurt my feelings! And you know that you're entitled to your opinions and you don't have to apologize for them—especially to me!"

Alyssa nodded and swallowed the lump that was forming in her throat. She knew her mom was right. In fact, her mom was always reminding her not to worry so much about other people all the time. But Alyssa also knew it had been a difficult decision for her mom to make, picking the family up and moving them hundreds of miles away to Florida. The only reason she'd done it was because she'd been offered a great new job down here. Alyssa knew that having a better job made things a lot easier for her mom, and at the end of the day, that was what mattered most. She never wanted to make her mom feel bad about her decision.

"You're right," Alyssa said finally. "Thanks for reminding me. And if I'm being totally honest, it does feel kind of weird that Christmas is just a few weeks away and we're wearing shorts. And I've barely seen any decorations in our neighborhood! Our street back home used to be filled with decorations a couple of days after Thanksgiving. I guess I'm just not feeling in the Christmas spirit yet—" Alyssa cut herself off, realizing she had used the term "back home." This was her home now. Palm Meadows. She looked carefully at her mom's face to see if she had hurt her feelings. But her mom didn't look upset. Her brow was furrowed, which was how she looked when she was deep in thought.

"You are absolutely right," Mrs. Sing announced, getting up from the couch. "I can't do anything about the warm weather, and I definitely cannot make it snow, but we need some Christmas spirit around here ASAP!"

"All right!" Alyssa cheered. "Let's kick off the holiday season, starting now!"

"What should we do for our holiday cheer kick-off?" her mom asked. "Our first trip to the mall to see the decorations and shop for presents? Or should we go get our Christmas tree?"

"Hmmm…" Alyssa thought about it. "Well, we should see what Cody thinks, but I'd vote for mall tonight and tree tomorrow."

"See what Cody thinks about what?" Cody asked as he walked back into the room.

Alyssa quickly explained that this weekend would be the official kickoff to Christmas for the Sing family. They were just deciding what should happen first.

"Well, I have that sleepover at Ben's tonight with a couple of other guys from the soccer team," Cody said. "I'd vote for you guys to go to the mall without me because, no offense, I'd rather be anywhere other than a mall." Cody settled on the other end of the couch. "And then tree tomorrow. I definitely want to be here for the tree."

"So it's all settled, then," their mom said happily.

Alyssa felt the tiniest pang hearing that her brother had a sleepover tonight. He'd been to at least three since school had started, and Alyssa hadn't even been invited to one. The truth was, she hadn't made any friends yet who were close enough to invite her over for a sleepover. She looked out the window and saw the sun reflecting off the bright green grass in their yard. She wondered what her friends in Massachusetts were doing tonight. Probably having a sleepover. During a blizzard. While watching Christmas movies.

Alyssa shook her head to clear it and turned her attention back to her family. Her mom was pulling sale circulars for the stores at the mall from the newspaper. And Cody was on his phone, looking up local places to buy a Christmas tree. In that moment, Alyssa felt her heart swell with love for her mom and brother. She knew how lucky she was to have such a great family. She squelched the pang of guilt she felt for missing her old home so much.

Chapter 2

After parking in the very crowded lot of the mall, Alyssa and her mom made their way toward the main entrance. Alyssa took in the red velvet bows adorning the palm trees that were scattered throughout the lot. The overall effect was...different. As if reading Alyssa's mind, her mom wrinkled her nose and said, "Bows on palm trees just isn't quite the same thing, is it?"

Alyssa laughed and nodded. "Let's hope things look more Christmassy inside!"

Moments later, they were delighted to see that the main entrance to the mall had been transformed into a winter wonderland! A display at the center of the entranceway showcased a snowy scene with fluffy snowmen surrounded by a candy-cane fence. A hand-painted sign said THIS WAY TO SANTA'S WORKSHOP!

Alyssa looked and could see Santa's Workshop in the distance, across from the food court. As she and her mom walked through the entrance hallway, Alyssa realized that Christmas carols were piping over the loudspeakers. Most of the individual stores had their own Christmas-themed signs and decorations adorning their front windows. A big grin lit up Alyssa's face.

"Okay, it's definitely starting to feel like Christmas now!" she told her mom, happily linking arms with her.

All around them, shoppers bustled about, their arms laden with packages. A big crowd was gathered at the coffee shop at the end of the hallway, and Alyssa was delighted to see that this shop had the same snowflake cups they had back home in Massachusetts every December. Her friends Ryder and Lauren always used to say it was officially the holidays once the coffee shop brought out the snow-flake cups. Alyssa made a mental note to tell Ryder and Lauren about the cups later. They might not have snow in Florida for the holidays but at least they had snowflake cups!

❄ ❄ ❄

"Look! Bookstore!" Alyssa told her mom, tugging her into the store. Books were one of Alyssa's favorite gifts to give. She already had an idea of what to get Cody—he was obsessed with video games and she knew there was a new book series out that was based on one of his favorite games.

"Mom, I'm going to head to the back of the store to look for something for Cody, okay?"

"Sure thing, honey," her mom replied. "I'll be in the cookbook section looking for a slow cooker cookbook for Aunt Sharon. That seems to be her latest cooking obsession."

"Ooh, good idea," Alyssa called over her shoulder as she headed back toward the kids' section. On her way there, a table of crafting books caught her eye. One book in particular jumped out at her. It was an advanced guide to knitting sweaters. Gorgeous, ornate sweaters, Alyssa realized as she flipped through the book. The patterns were really complex, but Alyssa knew someone who could tackle them—her friend from back home, Ryder, who was the best knitter Alyssa knew. He'd taught Alyssa everything she knew about knitting. Alyssa was a really good knitter, but Ryder was practically professional level—he'd even started the knitting club at Alyssa's old school. If anyone could manage an advanced sweater pattern, it was Ryder. She picked up the book and added it to the plastic basket she was carrying.

The book series Alyssa had in mind for Cody was easy enough to find—it was on display in the middle of the kids' section. Alyssa picked up the first book in the series and began reading the description on the back cover.

"Are you into that game?" a girl's voice asked.

Alyssa looked up and saw two girls her age standing in front of her. She recognized them from school but wasn't sure of their names. She was pretty sure they were best friends because they always ate together at lunch. The girl who had spoken to her was tall with red hair that she wore in a messy but effortlessly cool-looking bun on top of her head. The other girl had curly brown hair and big brown eyes.

"I'm Elle, by the way," the red-haired girl added a moment later. "And this is Rachel. Haven't we seen you at school? Palm Meadows? You're new? Alyssa, right?"

Alyssa felt a wave of different emotions all at once. Excitement that these girls were introducing themselves. Nervousness because she didn't know what to say or which question to answer first. And then complete and total awkwardness after she spoke.

"No," she blurted out. "I'm not."

"Oh…" Elle said slowly, a confused look flashing across her face. "Sorry, we thought you were this girl from our school. You look just like her."

"Oh, wait, I'm her!" Alyssa said quickly. "I meant

I'm not into this video game...." She held up the book she was holding. "It's for my brother. He's obsessed with this game, so I thought he might like the book." Alyssa realized she was speaking really fast. And kind of loud. "I was answering your first question," she mumbled.

Great job, Alyssa, she thought. *Some kids from school finally talk to you outside of class and you act like a total weirdo.*

But Elle and Rachel didn't seem to mind. In fact, they both grinned, and Rachel even laughed. "Don't mind Elle," she said cheerfully. "She likes to ask a million questions and confuses pretty much everyone she meets." She turned to Elle and playfully swatted her on the shoulder. "Stop bombarding the poor girl!"

Elle gave an exaggerated eye roll to Rachel, but then her grin got even wider. "Sorry about that. Rachel's right—I do ask too many questions! So, you are definitely Alyssa, right? From school? If you don't like video games, what do you like? How old is your brother?"

Alyssa and Rachel looked at each other, both on the brink of laughter.

"Oh, man, I'm doing it again, aren't I?" Elle added. Then all three of them burst out laughing.

As Alyssa caught her breath, she couldn't help but smile. Elle and Rachel were so easygoing and friendly! Alyssa couldn't remember the last time she'd laughed that hard with someone who wasn't her brother. *Probably not since we moved here*, she thought. Then she realized Elle and Rachel were looking at her expectantly.

"Right. Yes, I'm definitely Alyssa. My brother is Cody. He's in eighth grade."

"Is he here with you?" Elle asked, craning her neck to look around the store.

"No, he's at a sleepover with his friend from soccer. We're new, but he already has a ton of friends from soccer. I'm just here with my mom."

Way to point out you don't have any friends to hang out with on a Saturday night, Alyssa thought. *She asks me what I like, and I basically tell her I have no friends instead of answering her.*

"That's cool," Rachel said, and Elle nodded.

They must think I'm so boring.

"Well, I think my mom is waiting for me. I should go," Alyssa said a moment later. "But thanks for saying hi. I mean, it was nice meeting you," she mumbled. She felt her cheeks turning red and wished her hair was down so she could hide behind it like she usually did when she was feeling this embarrassed.

"We'll see you at school!" Rachel said cheerfully.

"I think we have the same lunch period," Elle added. "Hey, maybe you can sit with us on Monday?"

Alyssa couldn't believe it—they wanted her to sit with them even after she acted so awkwardly?

"I'd love that!" she said happily.

"Great, we'll see you Monday!" Elle said. "Oh, and you should totally get the book for your brother. I read the first two in the series, and they're really good."

With that, the two girls waved goodbye and walked away. Alyssa dropped the book in her basket and then decided to get Cody the second one, too. He deserved it for being the perfect icebreaker with the girls from school—even if he didn't know it!

After paying for her purchases, Alyssa joined her mom at the front of the store. They were both hungry and decided it was a good time to break for dinner.

Alyssa went to grab a table while her mom went to the pizza place to buy slices and sodas for each of them. Alyssa chose a seat across from Santa's Workshop so she and her mom could enjoy watching the little kids line up to get their photo taken with Santa while they ate.

"A slice of mushroom for me and a cheese slice for you," her mom announced a few minutes later as she put a plastic tray onto the table. "Plus one slice of white pizza cut in half for us to share, as always."

"Yum, thank you," Alyssa said, reaching for her slice.

Between bites of pizza, Alyssa's mom asked her about the girls she'd seen her talking to in the bookstore.

"They're from my school," Alyssa explained. "The red-haired girl is Elle, and the girl with the curly hair is Rachel."

"They seemed nice," her mom said after she finished chewing.

"Yeah, they were really nice, and really friendly, but I kind of clammed up." Alyssa put her piece of pizza down and wiped her fingers on a napkin. "I hate how awkward I get when I meet new people. When someone finally wants to be friends, I act all weird and shy."

"I'm sure you didn't act weird, honey," her mom said encouragingly. "And there's nothing wrong with being shy. Lots of people are shy. Including yours truly. I bet those girls liked you very much."

"Wait, did you say you're shy, too?" Alyssa couldn't believe it. Her mom was as confident and outgoing as Cody!

"You bet I am. Especially when I first meet new people," her mom replied. "Sometimes it just takes me a little while to warm up. I've always been like that." Her mom paused to take a sip of soda. "I haven't really made many friends at my new job yet. I miss having a friend to eat lunch with like I did at my old job."

"Wow, I never knew that," Alyssa said. "I thought people just flocked to you the way they do with Cody."

Her mom laughed. "Nope. Cody is one of a kind in that department. But you know what I find really helps me with my shyness? Not agonizing over it. If I'm a little shy or awkward when I meet someone new, I don't beat myself up about it. I remind myself that I know that the next time I see them, I'll feel a little more comfortable, and maybe before long I'll get to know that person enough that I can relax and be myself."

"Relax and be yourself," Alyssa repeated. She remembered how nervous she felt when she'd first started talking to Ryder and her friend Lauren at her old school. But then Ryder invited her to join knitting club, and soon she was really comfortable with both of them and Alyssa's shyness was a thing of the past. "Easier said than done," she said finally. "But maybe not impossible."

"To making new friends," her mom said, raising her cup of soda for a toast. "To *you and me* making new friends! Soon enough, we'll *both* have someone to eat lunch with!"

Alyssa clinked cups with her mom and then remembered that she actually *did* have lunch plans on Monday with Elle and Rachel. She told her mom, who clinked cups with her a second time.

"Listen to me giving you advice," her mom joked. "Maybe I should be asking you for tips instead!"

❄ ❄ ❄

About an hour later, Alyssa was all shopped out. She'd separated from her mom for a little bit so she could shop for her. Alyssa knew her mom loved candles, and she found a candle in the shape of a palm tree decorated with Christmas decorations. Even though it was a palm tree, it smelled like pine. It was silly, Alyssa knew, but she also knew her mom would love it. The perfect present to commemorate their first Christmas in Florida. As she waited at their designated meet-up spot, Alyssa noticed that the pet store had a sign in the window advertising animal adoptions. She checked her watch—she was a few minutes early. Definitely enough time to go check out the animals!

Alyssa loved all animals, but cats were always her favorite. Her mom had promised her she could get one when they moved to Florida and, true to her word, had asked a few times since they'd arrived if Alyssa wanted to go visit the local animal shelter to pick out a cat. Even though Alyssa wanted a cat more than almost anything, she had decided to wait until next summer to get one. She didn't want to bring a new pet home and then not get to spend a lot of time with it because she was at school all day. She'd be home all summer and could help her new pet get accustomed to its new home by being there for it. But there was no harm in looking!

Inside the pet store, there were about twelve cages, half with dogs and half with cats. Alyssa bee-lined over to a cage in the corner that contained three adorable kittens—two were black and one was orange.

"Hello, sweet babies," she cooed, sticking her finger through the bars of the cage to give one of the black kittens a gentle scratch on the head.

As she looked at the other cages, Alyssa noticed that some of them had cards that said HURRICANE RESCUE and wondered what that meant. She caught the eye of a woman who worked for the shelter and asked her.

"Those are pets who lost their homes due to recent hurricanes," the woman explained.

"That's so sad," Alyssa replied. "Is that what happened with these little kittens?"

"No, those kittens were found in Sunset Valley Park. We find stray cats there sometimes."

"That's right near where I live," Alyssa exclaimed, recognizing the name of the park that was just a few blocks from her home.

The woman nodded. "We care for the cats who live there, providing them with vaccinations and food, and we have a neuter-and-release program to prevent too many kittens from being born, but sometimes there are litters of new kittens. When we can, we try to find homes for the kittens."

"Why not all the cats?" Alyssa asked.

"Cats that have only known life outside often prefer it that way," the woman said. "That's what makes them happy. We just make sure they are cared for and fed."

With that, the woman excused herself to go talk to a family who had come in to adopt a dog. Alyssa smiled and took one last longing look at the kittens. She wasn't sure she could really wait until summer.

Chapter 3

The next morning, Alyssa woke up at her usual time but then decided to snooze a little longer. She'd stayed up pretty late the night before adding some embroidered finishing touches to one of the scarves she'd knit recently. Alyssa hadn't mastered all the complicated stitches that Ryder had taught her, but she had the basics down and enjoyed making her scarves extra special by adding embroidered details. Last night, inspiration had struck, and she'd decided to add snowflakes to the edges of one of her scarves. She tried to mimic the look of the snowflakes from the holiday coffee cups. She was really pleased with how the scarf had turned out.

Just as she was about to fall back asleep, something hit her: the smell of pancakes! That could only mean one thing—her mom was making her famous fluffy pancakes for breakfast! There was no way Alyssa was missing out on those.

"I was beginning to think I was going to be eating alone this morning," her mom said a few minutes later, when Alyssa came into the kitchen and plopped down at the table. Mrs. Sing looked over her shoulder from where she stood at the stove. "Did you sleep okay, sweetie? You look tired."

Alyssa explained that she'd stayed up a little too late working on one of her scarves.

"You know how important sleep is...." her mom began as she skillfully flipped a pancake.

"I know! It was a mistake. It won't happen again.... You know how much I love my sleep!" Alyssa replied.

"Well, if you want to go back to sleep for a little while, I can save some batter and make you a fresh batch of pancakes later. We don't have to leave for the holiday fair for another couple of hours."

"That's right!" Alyssa said excitedly. "I almost forgot today is the Palm Meadows Holiday Fair. I'm definitely awake now!"

Alyssa's mom chuckled as she slid a pancake off the spatula and onto the platter she had set on the counter next to the stove. Alyssa scanned the table and saw that her mom had already put down plates, juice cups, silverware, napkins, and, of course, maple syrup.

"Mom, you set three places. Cody is at his sleepover, remember?"

"He texted last night before bed to say Ben's mom offered to drop him off this morning on her way to do some errands. He should be home any minute now."

"I hope you made a ton of pancakes," Alyssa said dryly. "You know that boy has the appetite of three kids plus two adults."

As her mom set the platter of pancakes down on the table, Alyssa let out a squeal of delight—the pancakes were shaped like Christmas trees!

"Mom, these are so cool!" she exclaimed.

"Why, thank you," her mom said, pretending to bow. "I wanted to make something in the shape of a Christmas tree to celebrate us getting our tree tonight. I figured Christmas-tree-shaped pancakes were probably better than a Christmas-tree-shaped meat loaf!"

"Definitely better." Alyssa giggled as she took a big bite of pancake.

As they ate, Alyssa told her mom she was thinking about bringing a few scarves to sell at the fair. She'd been unsure about doing it until last night. She wasn't sure her scarves were special enough for someone to want to buy them, even though Cody and her mom kept telling her how nice they were.

"Which scarves are you bringing to sell?" Alyssa's mom asked.

Alyssa explained that she was bringing the green marbled one she'd added the embroidered snowflakes to, along with two others. Those three scarves were actually the only completed ones Alyssa had. Even though she spent a lot of her free time knitting, it took her ages to complete one scarf. And Alyssa was such a perfectionist with her stitches that she'd been known to work on the same scarf for weeks on end.

As Alyssa was asking her mom's opinion on how much she should charge for the scarves, Cody walked in the door. "I was thinking maybe thirty dollars for each scarf. Maybe a few dollars more for the one with the embroidery...." Alyssa was saying. "That covers the cost of the materials, and I still make a profit."

"I think more like five hundred bucks apiece sounds about right," Cody said as he set his backpack down by the table. "You put so much time into knitting one of those—people need to pay up! And then you can use the money to buy me a really awesome Christmas present."

"Ha-ha," Alyssa said, rolling her eyes at her brother. But she was secretly flattered that Cody thought her scarves were that nice.

"Guess what I just saw outside, near our driveway?" Cody asked as he settled down at the table, eyes on the pancakes. "A calico cat. It ran away when Ben's mom pulled up, but it was really cute."

Cody had barely finished his sentence before

Alyssa was out the door, scoping out the driveway for the cat. But it was nowhere to be seen. Disappointed, Alyssa came back inside.

"I wonder if she was a stray from the park," Alyssa said as she sat down at the table. She explained to her mom and Cody what she had learned from the woman at the mall the night before.

"That's cool that they take care of the stray cats," Cody replied. "That fluffy guy out in our driveway looked really well fed!"

"Oh, it was most likely a she," Alyssa told her brother.

"How do you know?" Cody demanded. "You didn't even see him!"

Alyssa grinned—she loved being able to teach her big brother something—and explained that most calico cats were female. Just like most orange cats were male.

"You sure know a lot about cats," Alyssa's mom commented.

"That's because she's obsessed with them," Cody grumbled.

Alyssa laughed. Her brother was right—she was just a little bit obsessed.

After helping himself to no less than three pancakes (even though he admitted to having had breakfast already at Ben's), Cody filled his mom and Alyssa in on his sleepover, explaining that he and the guys had spent most of the time playing soccer outside and then video games inside once it got too dark.

"Ben has a sister in your grade," Cody told Alyssa. "Her name is Becca. Do you know who she is? She thinks you have lockers near each other."

Alyssa nodded. "Yes, I know who she is. Long, light brown hair, usually in a ponytail? Green eyes?"

Cody scrunched up his face. "I have no clue what color eyes she has, but yeah, I guess that sounds like her. She plays soccer, on the girls' team. She came out and played with us. She's really good. Probably better than Ben, actually. She seemed pretty cool."

Alyssa nodded again. She definitely knew who Becca was. Alyssa never saw her talking to anyone other than the girls from the soccer team, so she'd had the impression that maybe Becca wasn't that friendly. Like she had her own exclusive club. But, Alyssa realized, that might've been an unfair assumption to make. If Cody said she was nice, then Alyssa was sure she must be. Maybe she'd even go up to her at school and introduce herself. Alyssa laughed to herself thinking that, for the second time, she could use Cody as an icebreaker.

❄ ❄ ❄

"I'm going to walk around a bit and think about it," said the woman who had been looking at one of Alyssa's scarves.

"Okay, thank you," Alyssa replied cheerfully even though she wasn't feeling very cheerful. The woman had been her first potential customer and had looked at the pink-and-blue scarf for at least ten minutes, trying it on and snapping pictures of herself wearing it. Alyssa had been sure she was going to buy it. But when Alyssa told her the price, the woman wrinkled her nose and said, "I'll give you ten dollars for it." Alyssa froze, unsure of how to respond. She didn't feel comfortable explaining to a grown-up why she believed her scarf was worth three times that amount. She didn't want to be rude! Luckily, Cody was standing next to her, and he jumped right in.

"That's actually a lot less than the cost of the yarn my sister used to knit the scarf," he explained. "She spends hours and hours on each scarf. Thirty dollars is a really great deal."

That was when the woman said she'd think about it and walked away.

"I don't know, Cody, maybe I am asking too much," Alyssa fretted to her brother. "I mean, I'm not a professional. I'm nowhere near as good as Ryder. Maybe I'm being delusional thinking people will want to pay thirty dollars for one of my scarves."

"Nonsense," Cody replied. "We just got here. Your scarves will sell. And if they don't, it's not because they're not worth it. It's because this is Florida and, well, let's face it...this place isn't exactly a winter wonderland, despite the best efforts of the Palm Meadows Holiday Fair committee to convince us otherwise."

Alyssa laughed and immediately felt her spirits lift. Cody was right about the effort the festival committee had put into making the outdoor market area look and feel festive. Holiday lights were strung up everywhere, and wreaths that had been sprayed to look as if they were covered in snow hung on the lampposts that dotted the path to the main part of the festival, where food and drink tables surrounded a big Christmas tree. There were tables selling hot apple cider, hot chocolate with marshmallows, and Christmas cookies. *They definitely get an A for effort*, Alyssa thought...even though she couldn't quite get excited by the thought of drinking hot chocolate outside on such a warm, sunny day.

Alyssa's thoughts were interrupted by the arrival of another customer—two, in fact. She looked up and realized she recognized these customers—Elle and Rachel from the mall!

"Fancy meeting you here," Rachel said, grinning.

Alyssa smiled shyly and gave the girls a little wave.

"Tell me you didn't make these," Elle said, eyes narrowed.

Alyssa felt her stomach drop. Did Elle think her scarves were terrible?

"I—I did make them," Alyssa murmured.

"Are you kidding me right now?" Elle demanded.

"What? Why? I . . ." Alyssa's voice trailed off.

"Ugh, Elle, stop with the drama!" Rachel scolded her friend. "What Elle here is trying to say is that these are amazing! You are so talented!"

"Absolutely!" Elle said, vigorously nodding. "Sorry, I didn't mean to sound bad. Like we told you last night—don't mind me. You'll get used to me and my brand of charm in time."

Alyssa's face broke into a huge grin as she allowed herself to exhale. "Thanks so much. I'm glad you like them. I worked really hard on them."

"That is so cool that you know how to knit!" Rachel replied as she ran her fingers over the green marbled scarf that Alyssa had added the snowflake embroidery to. "These totally look like something I'd buy online. How long have you been knitting for?"

Just as Alyssa was about to respond, Rachel's phone beeped. "Sorry, hang on one second," she said, scanning her phone screen. "It's my dad. He wants Elle and me to meet him for lunch. Can you join us, or do you need to stay here and try to sell your scarves?"

"I just got here a little while ago, so I probably ought to stay...." Alyssa said regretfully. She looked around to see if maybe Cody could take over for her for a bit, but he seemed to have wandered away.

"No worries," Rachel replied. "We'll come back later. Maybe my dad will buy one of your scarves for my uncle who lives in Alaska."

"We'll see you later!" Elle added with a smile.

Alyssa waved goodbye. *Did I just make friends?* she thought happily.

An hour later, a few more potential customers had stopped by to browse, but so far Alyssa had not made a sale. She'd received a lot of compliments on her scarves, though. *Maybe Cody was right*, Alyssa thought as she scoped out the stand next to hers to see how the proprietor's homemade jam was selling. *Maybe the scarves aren't the problem...but the year-round sunshine* is.

"Ooh, this is so cool. What do you think?"

Alyssa looked up and saw a pretty girl with long, light brown hair wrapping the green marbled scarf around her neck. She recognized her as Becca, Ben's sister. "It looks great on you," Alyssa replied honestly. "The green brings out your eyes."

"Thanks!" Becca beamed. "I love wearing green. I think it tricks my eyes into looking greener. When I wear brown, they look brown." She frowned, and then a panicked look crossed her face. "Not that there's anything wrong with brown eyes! Yours are nice! I mean, no offense!"

Alyssa laughed. "None taken."

Becca looked relieved. She tilted her head and looked more closely at Alyssa. "Wait, you're Alyssa Sing, Cody's sister, right?"

"That's me," Alyssa replied a moment later. She almost said "Guilty as charged," but had stopped herself, worried that sounded nerdy. There was something about Becca that made her a little nervous, but she wasn't sure why.

As if Becca could sense Alyssa's nervousness, she suddenly looked uncomfortable as well. Alyssa tried to think of something to say. "So, you're Ben's sister, then, right? Our brothers are, like, inseparable lately."

But Becca just nodded. "They so are. I think this was their third sleepover. Have you ever gotten stuck listening to them talk about video games?"

"Well, I haven't actually met Ben. But I have been stuck listening to Cody rampage about leveling up on his favorite game, so I can definitely relate," Alyssa replied, laughing.

The two girls fell into an easy conversation after that. And a few minutes later, Alyssa made her first sale! A man came up to her stand and said that his wife had mentioned admiring one of the scarves. "She doesn't know this yet, but I am taking her on a ski vacation in January. It's her Christmas present," the man explained.

"You should get the scarf and wrap it up with a little note telling her about the trip!" Becca exclaimed, thrusting the pink-and-blue scarf at him. "That way, she'll have something under the tree to open on Christmas morning!"

The man agreed that was a great idea, and Alyssa grinned at Becca. Her grin got even bigger when the man didn't bat an eyelash as Alyssa told him the price of the scarf.

"I owe you for helping me make that sale!" Alyssa said appreciatively as the man walked away with his purchase safely hidden in a brown paper bag.

"You don't owe me," Becca replied. "*But* I wouldn't say no to a Christmas cookie if you can take a break."

"Sounds good to me! Cody should be back in a couple of minutes, and I'll ask him to man the stand for me."

As Becca and Alyssa continued to chat, Alyssa caught sight of Elle and Rachel making their way toward her stand with a man who Alyssa assumed was Rachel's dad. Alyssa made eye contact with Elle, who was taller than Rachel, so her head stuck out above the crowd, and smiled and waved. Elle returned her smile. Alyssa felt a surge of excitement—she couldn't wait to introduce Becca to Elle and Rachel. Maybe all four of them could go have cookies together. But then something strange happened. As Alyssa watched them make their way toward her, she saw Elle's face cloud over. She stopped in her tracks a few stands away and said something to Rachel. Rachel frowned as she looked over. Moments later, Rachel waved apologetically at Alyssa and then turned and walked in the other direction with Elle, dragging her very confused-looking father away with them.

Becca, who had been talking about what she wanted for Christmas, stopped speaking as she noticed the crestfallen expression on Alyssa's face. "Is something wrong?" she asked, the concern obvious in her voice.

Alyssa wasn't sure what to say. What had just happened with Elle and Rachel? Were they mad at her for some reason? She didn't think that was it, but she couldn't shake the feeling that they had turned around when they saw her talking to Becca.

Alyssa knew she couldn't tell Becca that and was grateful when Cody showed up a moment later. "No, nothing is wrong. Let's go get those cookies."

Chapter 4

"Look, it fits perfectly!" Alyssa exclaimed.

It was a few hours later and after finishing up at the holiday festival, Alyssa, her mom, and her brother had headed to the local Christmas tree lot to choose their Christmas tree. In the past, the choosing of the Christmas tree had been far more complicated, as Cody and Alyssa usually chose different trees and their mom was stuck casting the deciding vote. She usually chose an entirely different tree to avoid playing favorites. But this year, the choice had been quick and easy. Alyssa spotted the perfect tree moments after they pulled into the lot. She ran over to it and declared, "This is the one!"

Cody took a long look at the tree and after a few moments slowly nodded in agreement. "Let us mark this momentous occasion," he announced dramatically. "Alyssa Sing has, for the first time in the history of Christmas, chosen the perfect tree!" he teased.

Now, back at home, everyone was happy to see how well the tree fit in the designated corner in the living room. In their old house, the tree always went in the entranceway, but this house was set up differently and didn't have enough space by the front door. But that was okay with Alyssa.... She liked knowing that the tree would be the first thing she saw every morning when she came downstairs.

While Cody went up into the attic to lug down the boxes of Christmas ornaments, Mrs. Sing got busy in the kitchen preparing a special surprise for them to enjoy while they were decorating. Alyssa wasn't sure what it was, but it definitely involved using the blender.

"No peeking," Alyssa's mom yelled when Alyssa appeared in the kitchen.

"I promise I'm not peeking!" And to prove it, Alyssa clamped her hand over her eyes and carefully made her way over to the door. "I just wanted to go outside and see if the kitty came back."

Outside it was nearly dark, but there was still enough light for Alyssa to look for the calico cat Cody had seen.

"Here, kitty, kitty," Alyssa called. "Are you out here? I'd love to meet you if you are," she said in her most friendly voice. Alyssa sat down in her driveway to wait and see if the cat might make an appearance. She'd read a lot of articles and books about cats and she knew they could be pretty picky about who they chose to spend their time with, but in her experience, cats almost always liked her. She just had a feeling this cat would, too. She waited silently, keeping her eyes and ears alert for any sign of the cat. A few minutes later, Cody stuck his head outside the door and announced that they were ready to begin decorating.

Back inside, Christmas carols were playing and Cody had put one of their favorite Christmas movies—*Elf*—on the TV with the volume off and the closed-captioning on. Mrs. Sing's surprise turned out to be frozen cocoa. It was like a cross between hot chocolate and an ice cream shake. More important, it was delicious. Alyssa had to fight the urge to chug the whole cup in one gulp, it was so good!

"This tastes like a delicious new holiday tradition," Cody commented as he nearly drained his glass.

"I'd like to propose a toast," Mrs. Sing said, raising her frosty mug. "To the Sing family Florida Christmas, new beginnings, and new traditions! May the laughter, light, and love of the season fill our hearts, and our new home, all year round!"

"Hear, hear!" Alyssa and Cody called in unison. They clicked their glasses together and then slurped up the last of their frozen cocoa.

Alyssa was sure that she was in for another new beginning at school tomorrow, too.

❄ ❄ ❄

An hour later, the tree was decorated. Alyssa, Cody, and Mrs. Sing stood back to admire their work.

"I think this is our prettiest tree yet," Alyssa observed. "The white lights really put it over the top."

"You say that every year," Cody teased. Just as Alyssa was about to protest, he held up a hand. "Let me finish! You say that every year, and this year you happen to be right! The white lights were a great choice. That's twice in one night you were right, Alyssa. It's a Christmas miracle," Cody deadpanned, throwing the pillow back at her.

"No throwing of the pillows, please," Mrs. Sing said, but she was chuckling. She excused herself to go finish up some work on her laptop.

The family ritual of decorating the tree together had been more fun this year than ever, Alyssa thought as she settled on the couch to watch the end of the movie with Cody. Between reminiscing about memories attached to the different ornaments and reciting lines from *Elf* while the movie played in the background, Alyssa couldn't remember the last time she'd had such a fun evening. It had helped to take her mind off of worrying about what had happened at the holiday fair. Now that she was thinking about it again, though, she couldn't help but wonder. She was really looking forward to having lunch with Rachel and Elle tomorrow... but what if they had decided they didn't like her anymore? At her old school, there had been some pretty complicated social dynamics between different kids, which made it hard to be friends with everyone. Alyssa had stayed out of all the drama—being best friends with Ryder and Lauren helped a lot because they just did their own thing—but Alyssa didn't really know what the deal was at Palm Meadows Middle School. She wondered if maybe there was some history between Rachel, Elle, and Becca. There had been some situations like that at her old school, where kids weren't friends in middle school because of something that had happened when they were younger. She hoped that wasn't the case... or that if it was, that whatever it was could be fixed. She wanted to be friends with *all* of them, and hoped maybe they could all hang out together. She didn't want to have to choose between her new friends.

Then again, she reasoned, maybe Elle and Rachel

didn't know Becca very well. Alyssa's first impression of Becca had been that she wasn't that friendly, when in fact she'd turned out to be one of the friendliest girls Alyssa had ever met. So maybe Elle and Rachel just needed to get to know Becca.

Alyssa stole a look at her brother as he sat at the other end of the couch, absorbed in the movie, even though he'd seen it at least a hundred times. She wondered if Cody might have some insight into the situation.

"Hey, can I talk to you about something?"

Cody hit pause on the remote and looked away from the screen. "Sure, what's up?"

Alyssa explained what had happened at the fair. "I'm positive Elle saw me, and I got the feeling that she and Rachel purposely avoided coming back to the table because Becca was there."

"Maybe they don't like Becca," Cody said, shrugging.

"Cody!" Alyssa exclaimed. "That's exactly what I'm worried about! What if that's true? I was hoping maybe they just don't know her. What am I going to do if they do know her and don't like her?"

"What *can* you do, Alyssa?" Cody tapped the remote control on his knee. "Who knows what their history is? Don't forget, they've probably known each other since they were really little. Maybe they had a fight in second grade because Becca stole their Play-Doh and they never got over it. You can't worry about these things."

Maybe Cody is right, Alyssa thought. She doubted if their conflict had to do with Play-Doh, but maybe something had happened in the past. Cody started the movie, and Alyssa grabbed the remote and paused it again.

"Can you ask Ben? Maybe he knows if something happened...?"

Cody sighed and looked at his sister. "Alyssa, I don't think it's your business—you barely know any of them. I also think you're '*getting way ahead of yourself.*'" He used air quotes at the end of the sentence because that was something their mom often said to Alyssa when she was worrying about something she couldn't control.

Don't get ahead of yourself, Mrs. Sing would say.

"I don't see why you're so worried," Cody said a

moment later. "I mean, Becca has friends from the soccer team, so you don't have to worry about her. It's not like you think Elle and Rachel are bullies or anything, do you?"

"No, definitely not," Alyssa said quickly. "At least, I hope not. They seem so nice. But so does Becca, and I just want to be friends with all three of them."

"Then you should be," Cody replied. "Elle and Rachel can't tell you not to be friends with someone. And if they do, then..." Cody sat up straight and waggled his finger at Alyssa in a bad imitation of a grown-up. "Then they're not really your friends after all."

Alyssa giggled as Cody tossed a throw pillow at her. "Look, just see what happens at school tomorrow. If it's really bugging you, tell them you don't want to be involved in any drama." With that, he turned the movie back on. It was almost the end, and Cody turned the volume up as the characters in the film sang "Santa Claus Is Coming to Town" to power Santa's sled.

Alyssa told herself Cody was right. There was nothing to worry about.

Chapter 5

"Your essays will be due on Friday the twenty-first,"
Mrs. Ramirez told the class. "That's the last day of
school before the holiday break. Now that might
seem like it's far in the future, but use your time
wisely. I want you to spend some time really thinking about the subject so you can write thoughtful,
heartfelt essays."

Alyssa wrote the date down in her notebook and
underlined it twice: <u>DUE 12/21</u>.

The assignment was to write about your holiday wish. Mrs. Ramirez told her students it could be
about anything they were wishing for, but that she

hoped the students would challenge themselves to come up with wishes that were in the spirit of the holidays and focused on things like friends, family, or helping others, rather than wishes for material things.

Parker James, a boy in Alyssa's class who was a bit of a class clown, raised his hand and asked, "Does that mean I can't write my essay about why I really, really *wish* to get a Nintendo Switch for Christmas?"

Mrs. Ramirez smiled patiently. "I would prefer if you wrote your essay about a wish that's a little more meaningful than that. It can certainly be something personal that you are wishing for yourself, but please let's try to avoid wishes for things like toys and clothes, okay?"

Alyssa didn't need to write that part down—there was no way she'd use her holiday wish for something like clothes. But the question was...what would she wish for?

Later that day, Alyssa walked into the cafeteria with a knot in her stomach. The knot had started forming at the end of fourth period, and now that it was lunchtime it was super tight. She hadn't brought her lunch with her, so she would have to buy it. But that wasn't what had her worried. She didn't know if she should go sit with Elle and Rachel, and that was the source of her concern.

She didn't have to think about it for very long because a moment later she felt a tap on her shoulder. It was Elle.

"Hey there! Rachel and I always sit right over there." She pointed to a table in the far corner of the cafeteria. "I'm going to get my lunch. Are you buying today, too?"

Alyssa confirmed that she was indeed buying, and the two girls headed to the hot-lunch line. Alyssa allowed herself to exhale. Elle was being so friendly. She certainly didn't seem to be upset with her.

While they were waiting, Elle asked her if she'd sold any of her scarves at the fair. Alyssa explained that she'd sold two—one to the man who was buying it as a gift for his wife, and then a second one right at the end of the day to an older woman who wanted to send it to her daughter in the Northeast as a Christmas gift.

After selecting their lunches—Elle promised that

the macaroni and cheese was the way to go—the two girls headed over to the table where Rachel was waiting for them. She'd already dug into her peanut butter and jelly sandwich.

Just be yourself and don't worry, Alyssa told herself. *Say whatever pops into your head.*

"We weren't allowed to bring PB&J at my old school," Alyssa told them as she took a tentative bite of her macaroni and cheese. It was actually really good. "There was a kid in my grade with a really bad peanut allergy, so we weren't allowed to bring any peanut products to school."

"Yeah, my cousin has the same thing at her school," Rachel replied. "Lucky for me, Palm Meadows is not a peanut-free zone because I could not live without my peanut butter sandwiches!"

Elle and Rachel asked Alyssa about her old school, and Alyssa told them all about Ryder and Lauren and their knitting club.

"You were best friends with a boy?" Elle's eyes widened. "What was that like?"

Alyssa shrugged. "I don't know.... It wasn't any different than being best friends with a girl. Ryder is just a cool person! And he started the knitting club at my old school and taught me everything I know about knitting. I guess we kind of bonded over our love of yarn," she joked.

"I get it. It's just a little different." Elle wiped off her apple with a paper towel. "But very cool," she added.

Rachel nodded in agreement. "Plus, you have a brother, right? So, you're used to being around boys."

Alyssa thought about that for a moment. "Yeah, I guess that makes sense. Cody is pretty cool, too, for an older brother. He's really into soccer. He made the school team...." Alyssa's voice trailed off at the mention of the school team. She wondered if Becca, who played for the girls' team, might come up. But Elle and Rachel just nodded and chewed. Alyssa tried to think of another way to bring Becca up. Their conversation switched to the essays about holiday wishes. Rachel and Elle weren't in Alyssa's class, but apparently the entire seventh grade had received the assignment. The girls began brainstorming ideas, when suddenly Becca appeared at the table.

"Hey, Alyssa," she said, a friendly smile on her face.

"Hi, Becca," Alyssa replied. She waited for Becca to say hello to Elle and Rachel, but she didn't. She looked at Elle and Rachel to see if they were going to greet Becca, but they both seemed to be staring very intently at their lunches.

"So, listen, I have some amazing news for you! Can we talk after school? Maybe we can meet after seventh period? I can take your bus home—I live, like, four blocks away from you. I just have to text my mom to let her know."

"Um, sure…" Alyssa thought she could feel the tension coming off Elle and Rachel in waves. This was so awkward! She swallowed and cleared her throat. "Do you want to sit down and join us?" she asked.

"Oh…" Becca's cheeks turned red.

Alyssa looked at Elle and Rachel, wondering for one terrible moment if they might say something. Alyssa didn't know what she would do if they told Becca she couldn't sit there. But they both remained silent.

"No, I sit at the soccer table. But thanks, anyway. I'll see you after class, yeah?"

Alyssa waved goodbye and waited for Elle or Rachel to say something. After a moment, it became clear they weren't going to say anything.

"So, maybe it's just in my head, but is there something up between you guys and Becca?" Alyssa asked, the words tumbling out of her mouth.

Rachel looked uncomfortable, and Elle sighed. "We used to be really good friends with Becca, and we're not anymore," Elle said finally. "The feeling is mutual—it's not like we ditched Becca or anything. We'd never do that," she added quickly. "It's a long story, but sorry if it was awkward."

"Yeah, sorry, Alyssa," Rachel repeated.

Alyssa nervously drummed her fingers on the table. She was relieved her new friends weren't bullies. But she was disappointed that her suspicions were confirmed—there was definitely some history between the three girls.

Across the cafeteria, Alyssa spotted the eighth graders filing in for their lunch period, which meant that seventh-grade lunch was about to end. Alyssa saw her brother come in surrounded by his friends from the soccer team. *Cody would tell me to speak up,* Alyssa thought. She stopped drumming her fingers and took a deep breath.

"Hey, um, I really like you guys, and I'm happy we're friends," she said finally. "But I also really like Becca. I hope there won't be any drama because I just want to be friends with everyone," she finished.

Alyssa waited a long moment for Elle or Rachel to respond. The two girls exchanged a look and then looked back at Alyssa, big smiles on each of their faces.

"No drama from us," Elle promised. "We're just glad you moved here!"

"Definitely," Rachel agreed.

Alyssa felt like she'd had a weight lifted off her shoulders, and she realized that the knot in her stomach was completely gone. Cody was right—speaking up really did feel pretty great!

Chapter 6

Becca was waiting for Alyssa near her locker after seventh period ended. She took the bus home with Alyssa but wouldn't tell her what the surprise was. She wanted to wait until they got to Alyssa's house. But Becca was lugging a huge paper bag, and Alyssa was pretty sure it had something to do with the surprise.

"That's my house up on the left," Alyssa said as they rounded the corner from her bus stop. Alyssa could see that on the side of the house, her mom's car wasn't in the driveway yet, but that was okay because Alyssa had a key. As Alyssa rummaged around in her backpack for the key, she saw her next-door neighbor outside in her garden.

"Hi, Mrs. Amir," Alyssa called, waving. "This is my friend Becca."

Mrs. Amir, who helped keep an eye on things for Alyssa's mom when she was at work, waved back and smiled. "Nice to meet you, Becca. Girls, I'll be right out here working in my garden if you need anything."

As Alyssa and Becca made their way inside and headed into the kitchen for a snack, Becca deposited the paper bag on the table and began to open it. Just when it seemed like she was finally going to tell Alyssa about the surprise, something outside caught her attention.

"You didn't tell me you had a cat!" she exclaimed.

"I don't!" Alyssa said, running to the window. Sure enough, the calico cat had made an appearance. In fact, she was sunning herself in the driveway!

Alyssa quickly explained the situation to Becca. "I don't know if she's a stray or what, but I have been dying to meet her. I can't believe she's out in the open like this, lounging in the driveway like she lives here! Do you think we should go meet her?"

"The two of us together might freak her out," Becca said after giving it some thought. "Why don't you go out there and see if she'll come to you?"

"Good idea." Alyssa nodded. "Wish me luck!"

Alyssa slowly made her way outside, sitting down in the grass a few feet away from the cat. She was even prettier than Alyssa had imagined she would be. Her coloring was beautiful. Instead of the traditional calico shades of orange, black, and white, this cat's coat had shades of pale gray, beige, and white. She looked so fluffy...and really well fed, just like Cody had said.

The cat eyed Alyssa as she approached. She looked a little nervous at first, and Alyssa worried she might take off, but when Alyssa stopped and sat down a few feet away from her, the cat seemed to get more comfortable. She stayed in her spot on the driveway, staring at Alyssa with her big yellow eyes.

"I'm Alyssa," Alyssa told the cat in her most soothing voice. "I live in this house, and I love cats. I just moved here. I'd really like to get to know you. If you're hungry, I can feed you."

Alyssa felt like the cat was listening to her as she

spoke so she went on. She'd read that it was good to talk to cats so they could get used to your voice. "I'm not sure if you're a stray or what. I don't see a collar, but you look very well fed. Do you live in the park?"

Just then, Alyssa heard her mom's car approaching the driveway. The cat heard it, too, and ran away. Alyssa stood up and dusted the dirt off her pants. "Bye, kitty!" she called.

"That was amazing!" Becca exclaimed as she ran outside. "You were so good with her. She totally loved you!"

Alyssa blushed happily. She had almost forgotten Becca was watching from the kitchen. Ordinarily, she might have felt silly talking to a cat in front of a girl she hardly knew, but Becca was just so warm and friendly that Alyssa didn't feel silly at all.

"Mom, this is my friend Becca from school," Alyssa said as her mom got out of her car. Mrs. Sing smiled warmly, and Alyssa realized how nice it had felt to say those words: *my friend from school.*

❄ ❄ ❄

A little while later, after polishing off a snack and chatting with Mrs. Sing for a bit, Becca was finally ready to tell Alyssa what her surprise was. She'd brought the paper bag up to Alyssa's room, where the two girls were sitting cross-legged on the bed.

"I want to see if you can guess, but I'll give you a big hint!" Becca opened the bag, reached her hand in, and slowly pulled out...a ball of yarn. "Ta-da!" she cried, tossing the ball of yarn to Alyssa. "And there's lots more where that came from! This bag is *filled* with yarn—every color plus some of the cool marbled kind!"

"You bought me yarn?" Alyssa asked. She was confused.

"Technically my aunt bought it," Becca replied, tossing a ball of purple yarn up and catching it. "Have you figured it out yet?"

Becca was so excited she was practically bouncing on the bed. She pulled more balls of yarn out of the bag and set them down. "You know about my aunt's store, right? I thought I told you about it at the fair, but maybe not...? Her store on Ocean Drive downtown? Near the pizza place? I know your brother knows about it because he met my aunt one of the times he was over hanging out with Ben."

Alyssa's head was spinning as she tried to follow along. Becca was talking really fast and reminding her a little of Elle. *Does Becca's aunt own a yarn store or something? Does she want to sell me yarn at a discount...?*

"So anyway, my aunt wants you to make scarves that she can sell at her store for the holidays! At first, she wanted them a *week* before Christmas, but I told her that might be asking too much and said December twenty-fourth was probably more realistic." Becca paused for a moment to take a breath and continued when Alyssa didn't say anything. "She'll take as many scarves as you can make with all this yarn. She thinks they'll sell really well because people love to buy accessories. Last year, she had these adorable little umbrellas, and they totally sold out. She'll pay you half of what she sells the scarves for. I thought that seemed fair since she was buying all the yarn, and she can buy you whatever needles you need, too...." Becca paused again and looked at Alyssa. Seeing the uncertain look on Alyssa's face, Becca's tone changed. "I hope this is okay. I mean, I told my aunt what a great knitter you were, and I thought this would be an amazing opportunity for you. But you don't seem very excited. Are you excited?"

Alyssa wasn't sure what to say or think. On the one hand, she knew Becca meant well. But on the other hand, this was a *lot* of yarn and Alyssa couldn't even imagine how many hours of knitting would be ahead of her if she agreed to do this. *But maybe Becca and her aunt don't know anything about knitting and they are only expecting one or two scarves....*

As if reading her mind, Becca said, "You could just do as many scarves as you could by December twenty-fourth. Maybe fifteen?"

"*Fifteen scarves?*" Alyssa croaked. Her throat felt dry. There was no way she could complete fifteen scarves in a year, let alone a few weeks.

"I can help," Becca said, nodding reassuringly.

"You could teach me to knit. I bet I'd be good at it. Not as good as you, of course, but how hard can a little scarf be, right?"

Alyssa felt her cheeks burn. She knew Becca wasn't trying to hurt her feelings on purpose, but those words stung.

How hard can a little scarf be?

"Alyssa, did I mess up here?" Becca asked, picking up a ball of yarn and squeezing it like a stress ball. "I know sometimes I go full steam ahead with stuff, and I don't mean to mow people over but then I do." Becca took a deep breath. "My friend Rachel…I mean, your friend Rachel, who used to be my friend…used to tell me that I mowed people over with my enthusiasm. I don't do it on purpose. I just get really excited about stuff. Just tell me if you don't want to do this and I'll take the yarn and go."

Your friend Rachel, who used to be my friend…

Becca's words echoed in Alyssa's head. She looked so sad. Alyssa could tell she missed Rachel. Of course she did. She probably missed Elle, too. Alyssa wondered what had happened to drive the friends apart. Did it have something to do with Becca "mowing people over"? But that sounded like something Elle would have a tendency to do, too, and Rachel seemed to have a good sense of humor about that, so Alyssa couldn't imagine that was what had broken up their friendship.

Alyssa took a deep breath and tried to figure out what she wanted to say. She definitely did not want Becca to leave, and she also didn't want Becca to feel bad. "It's okay. I'm not upset. I'm really flattered that you think my scarves are so nice and that you wanted to make this—opportunity—for me," Alyssa said slowly.

Becca exhaled loudly. "Oh, thank goodness!"

"I just…" Alyssa took another deep breath. "I just don't know how much time I'll have to work on all these scarves between now and then. I have the holiday-wish essay to work on and all my Christmas shopping…."

The words sounded lame, even to Alyssa. Was she "getting ahead of herself" again? *Why am I saying no automatically?* Alyssa thought. *Maybe I*

should be more like Becca and go full steam ahead instead of overthinking everything. I bet Cody would just say yes.

"That's totally fine!" Becca said. She looked happy again now that she knew Alyssa wasn't upset with her. "Like I said, you can teach me to knit and I'll help. We'll just do as many scarves as we can. Maybe we can even have a sleepover where we hang out and knit?"

Alyssa grinned. "Now you're speaking my language," she joked. "That sounds perfect. I just think we need to be realistic about how many scarves we can do in a couple of weeks. They take a long time...."

Becca nodded eagerly. "Whatever you say. You're the expert! But I bet we can make way more than you think we can!"

For the next hour, Alyssa showed Becca a few basic stitches. Becca picked them up quickly and seemed to have a real knack for knitting. They chatted as they practiced. Becca told Alyssa that she used to have a cat named Sprinkles. "She was the grumpiest cat ever," Becca said. "She didn't really like anybody except... well, she really liked Elle."

Alyssa wasn't sure what to say, so she nodded. "She must have liked you, too, since she was your cat."

Becca shrugged and laughed. "She *tolerated* me. I think the only human Sprinkles really liked was Elle. Rachel and I used to call Elle the cat whisperer because Sprinkles loved her so much."

Alyssa laughed, too. "Maybe I can get Elle to help me with the cat outside my house!" As soon as the words were out of her mouth, Alyssa regretted them. Would Becca think she was trying to brag that she was friends with Elle?

But Becca just nodded. "Yeah, you totally should. Cats love her."

An awkward silence followed, and Alyssa tried to think of something to say. Finally, she asked Becca about soccer.

"I actually don't love soccer all that much," Becca confided. "I hope this doesn't sound braggy, but I'm really good at it, so my parents kind of made me go out for the team. I was sort of hoping I wouldn't make it, but then I did."

"That doesn't sound braggy," Alyssa assured her.

"Cody told me how good you are." She carefully put down her knitting so she could really focus on what Becca was saying. "Have you tried talking to your parents about it?"

Becca sighed and continued knitting, her needles slowly clicking as she spoke. "It makes them so proud that I'm really good at something, and I don't want to disappoint them. It's not like I *hate* playing. It's just... a lot changed after I joined the team and I liked things the way they were before."

"What changed?" Alyssa asked.

Becca looked uncomfortable, and Alyssa instantly regretted asking. "I'm sorry, I didn't mean to pry," she said quickly.

"You weren't," Becca said kindly. "But would you mind if we maybe talked about something else?"

"Of course," Alyssa said. Alyssa had a feeling she knew what had changed so much in Becca's life since she joined the soccer team—her friendship with Elle and Rachel.

Moments later, Alyssa's mom called upstairs to let the girls know it was after five and she was wondering if Becca wanted to stay for dinner.

"Oh, I have to go—I promised my mom I'd be home," Becca said.

Alyssa showed her how to pause her knitting so she could pick it up again later. Becca decided to take half the yarn with her so she could work on some scarves. Alyssa bit her lip. "Becca, you definitely picked up those basic stitches really quickly, but I'm not sure you're ready to make a full scarf yet," she said gently.

But Becca just laughed. "Oh, don't worry—my aunt won't mind if some of them are more basic— they all don't have to be perfect like yours!"

Alyssa was pretty sure they would have to be perfect if her aunt wanted to sell them in her boutique, but she didn't feel comfortable disagreeing with Becca about it, since her aunt was the one who had paid for all the supplies. So instead of saying anything, she simply helped Becca pack up half the balls of yarn.

The two girls stood up, and Becca dashed off a text to her mom to let her know she'd be home shortly. Then she leaned over and gave Alyssa a quick hug. "I'm really glad you moved here, Alyssa," she said, a bright smile on her face.

Alyssa grinned, remembering that Elle had basically said the same thing to her earlier that day.

I'm going to figure out what happened between them and get them all back together, she promised herself.

Chapter 7

When Alyssa's alarm went off an hour earlier than usual on Thursday morning, she wondered for a moment why she'd set it so early before she remembered: She was waking up early to knit, just as she had done for the past two mornings. Her early-morning knitting sessions were paying off—she was almost halfway through one scarf so far. It was a simple stitch she was doing, but she was using different shades of red and pink to create an ombré effect. The ombré design had been Ryder's suggestion. They had FaceTimed on Monday night after

Becca had left, and Alyssa had filled him in on her new project. Ryder had been full of ideas for ways that Alyssa could design the scarves so they looked special without a ton of extra effort or complicated patterns.

It was great to talk to Ryder about what's going on with Becca, Rachel, and Elle, too, Alyssa thought. *He really understood why it's so important that I help the three of them get back together.*

"I would have hated to feel like I had to choose between you and Lauren," Ryder had said. "I think you're right—these girls just need a little push from their new friend, Alyssa, to help them see they belong together!"

Ryder's advice had been to try to come up with ways for everyone to spend time together. "That's kind of what happened with you and Lauren," he'd recalled. "Remember? I met you after I was already friends with Lauren. Then the two of you got really close after I started knitting club and you spent so much time together learning how to knit from the master," he'd joked.

Alyssa rubbed the sleep out of her eyes and smiled at the memory of her conversation with Ryder. Stretching, she glanced at the calendar on her desk. December 13. Just twelve days until Christmas. Eleven days until Becca's aunt needed the scarves for her store. Eight days until the holiday-wish essay for Mrs. Ramirez was due.

Don't get ahead of yourself, Alyssa thought as a tiny pang of worry about everything she had to do stirred inside her. When Alyssa wasn't worrying about making enough scarves for the deadline, she was actually enjoying the time spent knitting. Sometimes when she really got into a groove, her mind would wander while she worked. She'd given some thought to her holiday-wish essay, but most of the time her mind wandered to another topic: what she could do to fix things between Elle, Rachel, and Becca. She was sure that Ryder was right—if they just spent some time together, they'd realize that they could still be friends. Her plan had been to start small and see if they could all eat lunch together. Alyssa had eaten lunch with Elle and Rachel every day this week, but so far, she hadn't had the opportunity to ask Becca to join them again, since she was always sitting at the soccer table.

It might be time for plan B, Alyssa thought as she gathered the red ombré scarf from the basket on her dresser. She spread the scarf out on her bed and studied her work, looking for any loose stitches or mistakes. The scarf was coming along beautifully. She'd made more progress last night than she realized.

In fact, Alyssa had made a lot of progress on the scarf *and* with the calico cat the night before. After dinner, she'd gone outside with her knitting and sat on a lawn chair near the driveway, which seemed to be the cat's favorite spot. Alyssa had spotted her there the day after Becca's visit, and Cody had reported seeing her there one evening after soccer practice. She had taken to leaving a bowl of cat food out near the driveway every morning and was pleased to see that the bowl was always empty after school.

After about twenty minutes, Dasher, as Alyssa had begun calling the cat, had emerged out of the wooded area across the street and ambled over to Alyssa's driveway. She ate a few bites from the food bowl that Alyssa had just refilled and then lay down a few feet away from where Alyssa was seated and began to lazily clean herself. Alyssa grinned now as she remembered explaining to the cat why she was calling her Dasher—partly because it was the name of one of Santa's reindeer and partly because the cat seemed to like to dash away whenever she felt like it. It seemed to Alyssa that Dasher understood and even liked her name. She blinked her big yellow eyes at Alyssa and continued to contentedly groom herself. Before going inside, Alyssa got up from her chair very slowly and crouched down right next to the cat. She extended her hand and Dasher actually sniffed it! Alyssa held her breath and gave the cat a gentle scratch under her chin. Dasher stiffened up a little at first but didn't dash away. Deciding not to push her luck, Alyssa said good night and headed inside.

My mind is wandering again, and I haven't even started knitting yet, Alyssa thought. *I need to stop daydreaming and start knitting!* She gathered up the scarf and put it back in her knitting basket and decided to head downstairs to work in the living room. She padded down the stairs silently and set the basket on the coffee table. Then she plugged in the lights on the tree so she could enjoy their twinkling while she worked.

Alyssa quickly fell into a groove with her knitting. She was almost to the halfway point on the scarf and was determined to knit twelve rows of the raspberry color she was currently working with. This section of the scarf was where the reds would transition to pinks, and Alyssa thought the raspberry color was the perfect choice. She hoped Becca's aunt would agree! The next forty-five minutes flew by, and Alyssa almost couldn't believe it when she heard her mom's alarm go off. It was time to put the knitting away and get ready for school already!

❄ ❄ ❄

"That's the second time you've yawned so far," Elle told Alyssa at lunch later that day. "Was math class really that boring?"

"Sorry, I'm just tired," Alyssa replied. She put

down her tuna sandwich. "I've been waking up early to work on my knitting, and I think the lost sleep is just catching up with me. And if I'm being honest… math *was* pretty boring!"

"I knew it!" Elle laughed.

Just then, Rachel sat down, dropping her bagged lunch onto the table with a dramatic sigh.

"Everything okay?" Elle asked.

Rachel shrugged. Alyssa thought this might be the first time she'd ever seen Rachel without a big grin on her face.

"I got a seventy-eight on my Earth science test after studying for about a million hours. I was asking Mr. Jackson if there's some extra credit I can do." She opened her lunch bag and pulled out her peanut butter and jelly sandwich. "But he doesn't offer extra credit. He said I should just focus on doing better on the next test, but I don't know how I could study any harder than I already did!"

Alyssa nodded sympathetically. "I hate when that happens. Maybe you need a study buddy or a tutor? At my old school, they had this peer-tutoring thing and their motto was *Study smarter, not harder!*

My friend Lauren tutored kids in almost every subject because she was crazy smart." Alyssa took a sip of her cranberry juice. "I wish I could help you, but science isn't exactly my strongest class, either."

Elle drummed her fingers on the table, deep in thought. "Alyssa might be onto something here, Rachel. Maybe you can study with someone in your class who's doing really well? Studying *smarter* makes a lot of sense. Who's the top student in the class?"

Rachel picked up her sandwich and put it back down. Then she slowly peeled the lid off her yogurt before looking up again. "It's actually Becca," she said finally.

"Oh," Elle said quietly.

"That's perfect!" Alyssa said excitedly. She looked back and forth between her friends. "Ask Becca to study with you. I'm sure she would."

Elle and Rachel exchanged a look. "Yeah, maybe," Rachel said. But Alyssa had a feeling she didn't mean it. Before she could press her, Rachel changed the subject to ask Alyssa how things were going with Dasher.

"Have you lured her inside yet?" Rachel asked.

Alyssa wanted to talk more about Becca possibly tutoring Rachel but she sensed she shouldn't push it, so she explained that she hadn't lured Dasher inside yet but that she had managed to pet her a little bit.

"You need to get Elle over to your house ASAP," Rachel said as she swirled a spoon around in her yogurt. "Cats love her—I bet she could get Dasher inside."

"That's right! Becca told me how you're the cat whisperer!" Alyssa said. As soon as the words were out of her mouth, she wished she could pull them back in. *Is it okay I said that? I don't mean to keep bringing Becca up, but it's kind of hard not to....*

But Elle just grinned, seemingly happy to be reminded of her nickname, and Rachel laughed. "She's totally the cat whisperer!" Rachel cheered. "I say we get together at your house and see if Elle can help you get Dasher to come inside."

"I think we should make it a sleepover!" Elle added.

At that, Alyssa was beyond excited. Last week, she was sure she wouldn't make any friends in

Florida, but now she was being asked to her second sleepover of the week! But her excitement crashed quickly. What about all the knitting she needed to do? And her wish essay?

"Earth to Alyssa," Elle said, waving her hand in front of Alyssa's face. "You still with us? We were talking about a sleepover? Maybe this Saturday night?"

"I'm so sorry. I totally zoned out! Yes, let's do it!" Alyssa exclaimed. "I need to double-check with my mom to make sure it's okay, but I'm sure it will be. She used to let me have sleepovers all the time back home."

"Awesome," Elle and Rachel said in unison.

As the girls finished their lunches, Alyssa spotted Becca across the cafeteria at the soccer table. The kids were all goofing off, but Becca seemed to be in her own little world.

That's because she belongs over here with us, Alyssa thought.

And then she had a fantastic idea. She was going to invite Becca to her sleepover on Saturday night.

❄ ❄ ❄

Becca was waiting by Alyssa's locker after seventh period.

"Hey, are you coming over to knit?" Alyssa asked.

"No, I have soccer practice after school again, but I wanted to see if you wanted to have a sleepover on Saturday night? I checked with my parents, and it's fine with them. We can do it at my place or yours."

"Funny you should say that," Alyssa replied. She felt her heart beating excitedly in her chest. "I was going to ask you if you wanted to sleep over on Saturday night!"

"Great minds think alike!"

"Yes, they do!" Alyssa took a deep breath and chose her next words very carefully. "I hope you don't mind, but I also invited Elle and Rachel, so it would be the four of us." Alyssa watched in horror as Becca's face fell. "I know you guys aren't close anymore, but you're all my friends and I just think we'd have a lot of fun together!" Alyssa spoke so quickly that her words ran together.

"Do they know you're inviting me?" Becca asked.

"Well, no, not yet, but I'm sure they won't mind," Alyssa said quickly.

At least I hope they won't mind.

Becca looked at the ground for a long time. "You know what? I just remembered that I think I told Renee I would hang out with her on Saturday night to help plan some soccer stuff, so let's just do our sleepover another time," Becca said finally.

"But what about our knitting?" Alyssa said desperately. "We need to work on our scarves, remember?"

"Oh, I've finished four already." Becca waved her hand.

"Wait, what?" Alyssa forgot all about the sleepover for a moment. "How is that even possible?" she sputtered.

Becca just laughed. "I told you, I'm a fast learner!"

Alyssa shook her head in bewilderment. "I've been waking up early every day to knit and I've made half of one scarf. Do you not sleep?"

Becca laughed again. "I guess we work at different paces, but it's no big thing! I have to go to practice," she added. "But thanks again for the invite for Saturday. I'm sorry I can't make it."

As Becca jogged down the hallway, Alyssa wasn't sure what she was more confused about: whether Becca really had plans on Saturday night, or how Becca had finished four scarves already!

Chapter 8

"Someone's a hungry girl," Alyssa said softly as she watched Dasher practically inhale the bowl of food she'd just put down for her.

It was Saturday morning, and Alyssa had allowed herself to sleep in because she'd made a lot of progress on the ombré scarf the night before. She'd sat outside under the stars with Dasher lying at her feet, purring contentedly while Alyssa knitted. Alyssa explained to Dasher that it was Christmastime and told her that she used to associate Christmas with cold weather and snow, but now that she lived in Florida she was beginning to realize that the season was so much bigger than just the weather.

Then Alyssa had told the cat all about what was going on at school with Becca, Elle, and Rachel. Dasher, of course, didn't have any advice to offer, but Alyssa felt better after having talked about what was on her mind. She had also decided that maybe it was time to talk about it with someone who could actually give her advice about what to do . . . and she knew just who the perfect person was.

"I'm going inside now for a bit. Okay, Dasher? I think it's time to talk to Mom about all that drama I told you about," Alyssa told the cat as she continued to devour her food. "But my friends Elle and Rachel are coming over later and they are really excited to meet you!"

Dasher looked up from her bowl and blinked her eyes slowly at Alyssa. Alyssa smiled. She was positive Dasher understood every word she was saying.

Back inside, Alyssa fixed herself a bowl of cereal and sat down at the kitchen table. Mrs. Sing had just returned home from her run. "Are you excited about your sleepover tonight?" she asked as poured herself a glass of cold water and joined Alyssa at the table.

"So excited." Alyssa nodded happily. "But I wish Becca could come, too. I invited her and she said she couldn't make it."

Mrs. Sing drained her glass and put it on the table. "Do you think she wasn't being honest with you?"

"No…I mean, I'm not sure." Alyssa explained to her mom that there was some history between Elle, Rachel, and Becca and they were no longer friends but that she was determined to bring them all back together.

Mrs. Sing frowned. "That's tricky territory, honey. Are any of them making you feel like you're caught in the middle of this…misunderstanding…they've had? Do they say things about one another to you? Because that would not be fair to you.…"

"No, not at all," Alyssa said quickly. She could tell her mom was concerned, and she didn't need to be. "I actually talked about it a little with Elle and Rachel and *told* them I wanted to be friends with everyone and they promised me that was fine with them and they haven't *ever* said anything bad about

Becca. Just that they used to be friends and aren't anymore." Alyssa paused to take a bite of her cereal. Her mom was still frowning a little bit. "And Becca has also been great about it, though I do think she turned down coming to the sleepover because Elle and Rachel will be here."

Mrs. Sing absently traced her finger along the rim of her empty glass. "I'm glad they aren't trying to involve you. They sound like good friends."

"Oh, they are," Alyssa agreed.

"Do you know what happened, why they aren't friends anymore?"

"No, but I'm going to try to find out tonight. I think if I knew what drove them apart, I could help fix it and they can make up."

"Alyssa, it's not really up to you," Mrs. Sing said gently. "I know you want to help, but you're just getting to know these girls. Why don't you try to focus on that for now? If they are meant to be friends, they will be, but you can't force it." Her voice grew even softer as she reached out and squeezed Alyssa's hand. "Sometimes friends just grow apart. It's difficult, but it happens."

Alyssa felt her cheeks burn. She wasn't explaining it correctly to her mom if it sounded like she was trying to *force* them to be friends. "No, Mom, it's not like that," Alyssa said firmly. "I'm telling you—I just *know* they should all be friends. I can't explain how I know, but I just do. Kind of like how I just know Dasher is supposed to be my cat. And I want to be friends with all of them—I don't want to have to choose."

Mrs. Sing put her arm around Alyssa and gave her a side hug. "I love that you care so much about other people, sweetie. Just make sure you allow yourself to enjoy getting to know your new friends and not worry so much about everything else. Okay?"

Alyssa nodded, but she wasn't sure her mom really understood what she was saying. *Of course* she was enjoying her new friendships, but she would enjoy them even more once everyone was friends with one another.

❄ ❄ ❄

"Don't look now, but I spy a furry calico cat...." Elle whispered.

"Why are you whispering?" Rachel demanded as she ran over to the kitchen window.

"I don't want to startle the cat and scare her away!"

Rachel and Alyssa burst out laughing.

"Pretty sure she can't hear us all the way in here," Alyssa said. But as she said it, Dasher seemed to look over from the driveway. "Or maybe she can hear us! You really are the cat expert, aren't you?"

Elle put down the spoon she'd been using to stir the cookie batter. "Yes, I am. And you should just always assume I know exactly what I am talking about, thank you very much!"

Mrs. Sing laughed along with Alyssa and Rachel as she walked into the kitchen to check and see how the baking was coming along. "Okay, so Dasher has made her appearance. What's the plan?"

Everyone looked expectantly at Elle.

"Well, I've given this a lot of thought," Elle began. "I think Alyssa should just go outside and say hello to Dasher and then come back inside but leave the door open so Dasher knows she's welcome to come in. We can all pretend to ignore her, and she can come in and get comfortable without feeling pressure from any of us."

Alyssa, Rachel, and Mrs. Sing considered Elle's plan.

"I think that's a great idea," Alyssa said, and her mom nodded. "Wish me luck!"

A few minutes later, Alyssa returned to the kitchen. Rachel and Elle were hovering by the kitchen window. "You were so good with her!" Elle squealed. "I can tell she really likes you."

Alyssa grinned as she remembered that Becca had said almost exactly the same thing to her a few days ago. That had a tendency to happen.

"Is she coming yet?" Mrs. Sing asked.

"No, but she's definitely looking," Rachel reported.

"Why don't you girls get back to working on the cookies, and I'll keep an eye on the door and let you know if there's any movement?" Mrs. Sing said as she settled at the kitchen table and opened her laptop. "The oven is heated up and the cookie sheets are greased. Just don't forget to set the timer," she added, winking at Alyssa.

Alyssa started telling her friends about the time she was making sugar cookies and forgot to set the timer. "This was in our old house in Massachusetts and I was in the den waiting for the timer to go off but it never did. And then—"

"Girls!" Mrs. Sing loud-whispered. "Dasher appears to be on her way in."

The calico cat poked her head inside the door. As soon as she stepped into the kitchen and spotted all the humans, she froze. Alyssa and her friends quickly got back to work, pretending not to notice the cat.

"Does this look like it's stirred enough?" Alyssa asked, holding her bowl up.

"Alyssa, I don't think she actually understands what you're saying." Rachel giggled.

Alyssa said, "She does so!" at the exact moment Elle said, "Of course she does!"

All three girls burst into laughter and, true to her name, Dasher dashed! But instead of dashing out the door, she dashed through the kitchen and up the stairs!

It took every ounce of patience Alyssa had to finish working on the cookies with her friends instead of running through the house to see what Dasher was doing, but she did it! Finally, after about half an hour of kneading, rolling, and cutting out dough, the cookies were baking in the oven. Mrs. Sing promised to keep an eye on them while Alyssa, Rachel, and Elle went upstairs to see what Dasher was up to.

Alyssa almost couldn't believe her eyes when she got to her bedroom and saw Dasher curled up on her bed, sound asleep on her pillow.

"Aw, she knows she's home," Elle said softly. "This means she's chosen you as her person," she added. "She must feel really safe with you."

Alyssa slowly approached the cat, who opened her eyes as soon as Alyssa got close. "It's okay, Dasher—don't dash away from me," she said gently, holding her hand out so the cat could sniff it. Then she stroked the cat's chin and, to her delight,

Dasher lifted her head up and accepted the chin rubs. A moment later, she rolled over onto her side and showed her big white belly. Alyssa knew enough about cats to know this was the ultimate sign of trust—Dasher *was* meant to be her cat!

Alyssa glanced at Elle and Rachel as they watched happily from Alyssa's doorway.

"Look at how much she loves you," Rachel cooed.

"She really does, Alyssa," Elle agreed. "I think this was definitely meant to be."

Alyssa sat down on her bed and continued to run her fingers through Dasher's silky fur. "I think this might be the chubbiest cat I've ever seen," Alyssa said.

"I was just thinking the same thing," Elle agreed.

"She's not fat...she's just fluffy!" Rachel cooed.

Elle and Alyssa laughed.

"I can't believe how comfortable she is with you," Elle said as she gingerly sat down on the bed next to Alyssa. Dasher watched her closely but didn't change her position.

"I think it was all the time I've spent talking to her this week," Alyssa said as she rubbed Dasher's expansive tummy. "She knows my voice."

"It's more than that," Elle said. "She knows she's home."

"The cat whisperer has spoken," Rachel added.

Alyssa felt her heart swell with joy as she smiled down at her cat.

"Welcome home, Dasher."

Chapter 9

"If I eat one more cookie, I am going to explode," Rachel declared. "I am too full to ever eat again!"

"Me too," Elle agreed, rubbing her stomach for emphasis. "I should have stopped after *Home Alone 2*," she joked. "Those were the best sugar cookies I've ever had. You were totally right about adding a pinch of brown sugar."

Alyssa smiled happily from her spot on the floor of her bedroom. They had just finished watching *Home Alone 3*, the third movie in their holiday movie marathon. Dasher was curled up next to her, purring contentedly while she napped. "I can't take credit for the cookies. It was my mom's recipe. She's an amazing baker. I'm actually kind of a terrible baker unless I follow a recipe."

"Well, you can't be any worse than—" Rachel stopped speaking suddenly.

"Than who?" Alyssa prompted.

"I think she was going to say Becca," Elle finished. Rachel nodded. "We used to have a holiday sleepover every year, just the three of us. We'd been doing it since second grade, and so we had a bunch of traditions." Elle began to pet Dasher gently as she spoke. "One was making a million Christmas cookies. Becca would somehow mess them up. *Every* year. It was kind of hilarious. Baking is, like, the one thing she's not good at."

"We're not making fun of her when we say that," Rachel added quickly. "You can ask her—she'd tell you herself!"

"Oh, it's okay, I didn't think you were being mean," Alyssa replied. Dasher woke up, stretched, and curled back up into a ball, moving even closer to Alyssa. "Speaking of Becca... I had invited her to come tonight," Alyssa said quietly.

For a moment, neither Elle nor Rachel spoke, and Alyssa felt a knot form in her stomach. *Are they angry I invited her? Say something!*

Elle spoke first.

"What did she say?" she asked.

"She said she couldn't make it," Alyssa replied uncomfortably. *Why did I bring it up this way? This is just awkward.* "She had plans with Renee...?"

"Renee is one of the girls from the soccer team," Rachel said. "One of the girls Becca is really friendly with now...now that she's not friends with us anymore."

The air grew thick. Alyssa hated how uncomfortable things became whenever Becca came up. She took a deep breath and blurted out what she had been wondering for a week now. "What happened between you guys?"

Elle and Rachel exchanged a look. Rachel shrugged and nodded to Elle.

"At the beginning of last year, Becca went out for soccer," Elle began. "She made the team. She's really good...."

"*So* good," Rachel interjected.

"And the kids on the soccer team are really close," Elle continued. "They have their own parties and sleepovers and stuff...."

Alyssa nodded. "Yeah, my brother is on the boys' team and he's always doing things with the guys from his team."

"Exactly." Elle nodded. "And I guess Becca just liked hanging out with the soccer kids more than us because before long she just stopped spending any time with us. She came to my birthday party that year, but she showed up an hour late and then had to leave early because there was some soccer team emergency."

"And then she bailed on our annual holiday sleepover," Rachel added sadly. "She called at the last minute to say she couldn't make it because of some soccer party. And then when we returned to school after the holiday break last year, she stopped sitting with us at lunch so she could sit at the soccer table. No explanation or anything. She just stopped being our friend."

Alyssa looked at her friends' faces, and she could tell it was hard for them to talk about it. They missed Becca—she was sure of it.

"I'm really sorry that happened," she said finally. "I have to say, though, that does not sound like the Becca I know. I mean, she's busy with soccer for sure, but she's been making all this time to help me knit scarves for this insane scarf order I have. She's being a really good friend to me...."

"She's a great friend to have," Rachel agreed. "She just stopped wanting to be *our* friend. My mom said that sometimes friends grow apart, and that's what happened, I guess."

"I just can't believe that," Alyssa said honestly, even though her own mom had told her basically the same thing. "She doesn't seem like the kind of friend who just...discards her old friends when she makes new ones."

"Or maybe she just got tired of us," Elle said simply. Alyssa started to protest, and Elle held up her hand. "Hey, it's okay, Alyssa. You are awesome and I don't blame Becca for finding room in her busy schedule for you. She just never made time for Rachel and me after she joined the soccer team. It's like she decided she wanted to move on, and she did."

Alyssa was positive that *wasn't* what happened, but she knew she couldn't keep disagreeing with Elle.

"It's okay, Alyssa," Elle continued. "Rachel and I have each other, and now we have you, too, as our friend."

"Right," Rachel said.

Alyssa twirled her fingers in Dasher's fur. "Thanks for saying that—I'm so glad you guys are my friends! But I have to tell you, I think you're wrong about Becca. I think this was all just a misunderstanding. I can't explain it, but I really think she misses you."

"Has she said that?" Elle asked.

"Not exactly," Alyssa admitted. "It's just a feeling I get. I feel like if she could have come tonight we all would have had so much fun. You guys remind me so much of each other," she added, looking at Elle.

"OMG, tell me about it." Rachel laughed. "I used to say that all the time."

Elle smiled, too, at the memory. "Maybe you're right," she said finally. "I miss Becca, and I'd love to be friends with her again," she added. "I've just never thought that maybe she missed us, too...."

"Me neither," Rachel said softly.

"I have an amazing idea, then," Alyssa said, jumping to her feet so fast she startled Dasher. "Let's have a do-over sleepover next weekend with the four of us!"

"Actually, about next weekend..." Rachel began. "Elle and I were planning to have our annual holiday sleepover on Saturday night...."

"Oh. Right," Alyssa said. She felt her cheeks burn with embarrassment. "That's okay. We can do it some other time."

"Alyssa, let me finish!" Rachel said playfully. "Elle and I already talked about it, and we wanted to invite you to come this year! And maybe...well, maybe we can invite Becca, too...." Her voice trailed off as she looked at Elle uncertainly.

"I don't know," Elle said, replying to Rachel's unspoken question about Becca. "First things first... Alyssa, will you come to our sleepover next weekend?"

"Definitely!"

"Great. And as for Becca, Rachel and I will sleep

on it. Maybe we can talk to her at lunch next week or something and see how it goes. I'm all for giving this a chance if she wants it, too, but we need to know that she actually does want it. Is that fair?"

"Totally fair," Alyssa replied.

A short while later, Alyssa was curled up in bed with Dasher beside her. She could tell Elle and Rachel were asleep from their even breathing. Alyssa sighed happily and snuggled with Dasher. She'd had the perfect holiday sleepover tonight and had plans for another one next weekend... one that would hopefully include *all* her friends.

As Alyssa drifted off to sleep, she realized she knew exactly what she wanted to write her holiday-wish essay about. She just hoped it was okay to write about a wish that had already come true.

Chapter 10

"I thought you said last night that you were too full to ever eat again," Alyssa teased Rachel as she reached for another waffle.

"I know, but my appetite miraculously returned overnight," Rachel explained. "Besides, your mom's waffles are *so* good!"

It was late Sunday morning. The girls had slept in and were enjoying a lazy breakfast. Dasher wandered into the kitchen, as if to see what the girls were up to, and when she determined the girls were too busy eating to pay attention to her, she wandered back out.

"I can't believe how quickly she made herself at home," Rachel commented.

"Yeah, she even found the litter box we set up for her and used it like a champ," Alyssa replied. "It's so hard to believe she was a stray...."

"Alyssa, speaking of that..." Elle shifted uncomfortably. "I was thinking, what if Dasher belongs to someone and she just got lost or something? Maybe you should call the animal shelter and find out if anyone reported her missing."

"My mom already talked to me about that," Alyssa replied. "She's going to take Dasher to the vet next week to have her checked out, and they can check to see if she was microchipped. If she was, they can scan her microchip and find her family." Alyssa's voice wavered a little bit as she said the last part. *I don't know what I'll do if that happens*, she thought. She knew her mom was right, that they had to make sure Dasher was really theirs to keep, but the thought of finding out she *couldn't* keep her was just too upsetting to think about, so Alyssa was trying very hard not to.

"She definitely belongs with you," Elle said kindly.

"Agreed." Rachel nodded. "She might have belonged to someone else before, but why aren't they looking for her, putting up flyers and all that? Or I bet she ran away because she wanted to live with you instead and her owners know they've been rejected!"

Alyssa laughed. Her friends definitely knew how to make her feel better.

Just then, the doorbell rang. "I'll get it," Mrs. Sing called from the den.

A few moments later, Ben, Becca's brother, darted through the kitchen on his way up to Cody's room. "Hi, bye!" he called as he sped past the table.

Mrs. Sing popped her head into the kitchen. "Alyssa, Becca is here, too. She came with Ben. She realized you have guests, and she's saying she wants to leave so as to not interrupt you...." She gave Alyssa a look, but Alyssa didn't even need for her mom to tell her what the right thing to do was. She glanced at her friends, and they both nodded.

"Becca, get in here," Alyssa called. "We're just finishing up breakfast, but there's still plenty of food if you're hungry."

Mrs. Sing smiled and excused herself as Becca walked into the kitchen. Alyssa thought Becca looked nervous and realized that she felt pretty nervous herself!

"Hi," Becca said slowly. She stood awkwardly by the table. "I'm sorry to interrupt. I just came by to see if you wanted to work on some knitting, but you're busy. Should I come back later?"

Elle spoke before Alyssa had a chance to reply. "Like Alyssa said, look at all this food. Why don't you join us?"

Alyssa knew from the grin that lit up Becca's face that she had been absolutely right—Becca did miss Elle and Rachel and wanted to be friends again. Alyssa was sure of it.

Becca set her bag of knitting down on the end of the table and took a seat. "Yum, waffles!" She reached for a plate. "Still your favorite breakfast, Rachel?"

"You know it," Rachel said. "I am currently trying to decide if my stomach can handle a third one or not...."

Alyssa, Becca, and Elle laughed.

"Ooh, is that the calico cat from outside?" Becca asked suddenly, eyes wide. She pointed to Dasher, who had wandered back into the kitchen.

"Yep, she came inside last night," Alyssa replied. She explained how they had lured Dasher inside by leaving the door open and how she had slept by Alyssa's side all night.

"Are you allowed to keep her?" Becca asked.

"Hopefully…" Alyssa recounted how her mom would be bringing Dasher to the vet and they would check for a microchip.

"She definitely belongs with you," Becca said firmly.

"That's exactly what we said," Elle replied.

And just like that, the girls were laughing and chatting like the old friends they were. Alyssa got up from the table to refill Dasher's food bowl and to give her friends a chance to chat for a few minutes. *This is going even better than I ever imagined it would*, she thought excitedly as she measured out some cat food. Dasher weaved herself around Alyssa's ankles; she clearly understood what Alyssa was doing!

"Be right back. I have to go use the bathroom," Becca said as Alyssa returned to the table.

Alyssa snuck a look at her friends' faces, and they were both relaxed and smiling. There was no tension at the table at all. Alyssa sighed happily and began picking at some of the fruit left on her plate as Cody and Ben came into the kitchen.

"Are there any cookies left over, or did you guys eat them all?" Cody demanded.

Alyssa rolled her eyes and pointed to the plates of cookies on the counter. "Of course we didn't eat them *all*," she replied. "We just ate...a *lot* of them."

"Hey, Ben, I was trying to explain to Alyssa last night just what a big disaster Becca is in the kitchen when it comes to baking," Elle said, giggling. "Do you remember that time she used a cup of salt instead of sugar? I was joking that it was a good thing she wasn't able to join us last night. She probably would've contaminated the cookies!"

Ben laughed as he took a giant bite of a cookie. "Ugh, she's the worst baker ever!" he agreed. "But why couldn't she join you last night? She was just sitting home doing nothing."

"I thought she was at Renee's?" Elle said.

Alyssa felt her stomach clench as Becca returned to the kitchen. She seemed to sense that she'd walked in on an awkward conversation.

"Why did they think you were at Renee's last night?" Ben asked his sister. "You haven't hung out with her in forever."

When Becca didn't answer, Ben just shrugged and grabbed a handful of cookies. Cody exchanged a sympathetic look with Alyssa and pulled his friend out of the kitchen.

Becca returned to her seat at the table. Her head was down, but Alyssa could see that her cheeks were red.

"So you stayed home last night instead of coming to Alyssa's sleepover?" Elle asked finally, her tone frosty.

"Alyssa said you had plans with Renee," Rachel added.

Alyssa wanted to say something—anything—but didn't know what to say.

"I made that up," Becca said finally. "I made it up

after Alyssa told me you guys were going to be here because—"

"Because you didn't want to spend time with us," Elle interrupted.

"No, that's not true," Becca cried.

"We're sorry that we're so horrible to spend time with that you have to make up excuses to avoid sleepovers with us," Elle snapped.

"Elle!" Alyssa exclaimed. She knew Elle was upset, but that didn't mean it was okay to speak so harshly to Becca.

"Alyssa, don't you see?" Elle's voice rose. "She *lied* to you. Are you really okay with that? I mean, what kind of friend lies about having plans to avoid spending time with you?"

Alyssa didn't know what to say to that. She knew it was wrong that Becca had lied, but she also knew she had probably done it because she was afraid Elle and Rachel didn't want to spend time with her.

"She's right, Alyssa," Rachel said sadly. "It's never okay to lie to your friends...."

"I know, but..." Alyssa's voice trailed off as she

tried to think of a way to fix what was happening. She didn't want to say anything that would make the situation worse.

"I should just go," Becca said. She stood up from the table and grabbed her bag of knitting. "Alyssa, I'm sorry I lied to you." Becca's hair fell over her face, but Alyssa was pretty sure she saw teardrops on her cheeks. "I'll just talk to you later…about the knitting…if you still want to talk to me, I mean." With that, she fled from the kitchen.

"What was that?" Alyssa asked, turning to Elle. "You made her cry! You didn't even give her a chance to explain!"

"Are you seriously siding with her right now?" Elle demanded. "Alyssa, she *lied* to you. Friends don't lie!"

"I know that," Alyssa said, trying to keep her voice even. "But I think she lied because she thought you guys wouldn't want to spend time with her."

"So it's our fault?" Elle got up from the table. "I'm going to go text my mom and see if she can come pick us up."

Alyssa sat down at the table and looked at Rachel, who looked as upset as Alyssa felt.

"She's not really mad at you," Rachel said quietly. "She gets really upset—as you just saw—and does *not* choose her words carefully. Once she calms down, I promise she will apologize."

Alyssa sighed. She felt like her head was spinning.

"I just don't understand why she's so convinced that Becca was being a bad friend to *me*. I mean, I don't love that she lied to me, but I think it's pretty obvious she thought she was doing the right thing because you guys aren't friends anymore...."

Rachel bit her lip and looked like she wanted to say something but was holding back.

"What?" Alyssa asked. "Tell me what you're thinking."

"It's just..." Rachel shifted uncomfortably. "What if Becca doesn't really want to be friends with you and she's just... *using you*?"

"Using me for what?" Alyssa exclaimed.

"The knitting stuff," Rachel replied. "She had you teach her how to knit, right? Maybe she wants to learn to knit so she can make stuff to sell, too. She came over this morning to knit with you, after she told you she couldn't come to a sleepover last night...."

Alyssa shook her head. "No way. That's not it. She's my friend." But as she said it, a tiny doubt crept into her mind. *Maybe Becca doesn't really want to be my friend. Why would she want to be my friend when she has all those friends from the soccer team?*

Alyssa sat in silence with Rachel until Elle came back into the kitchen holding her overnight bag and Rachel's. "My mom is on her way," she said quietly.

Alyssa nodded. She picked up her fork and began poking at the hardened maple syrup on her plate.

"Alyssa, I'm really sorry," Elle said, sitting down next to her. "I'm sorry I lost it and yelled at Becca... and you. It just really hurt when she ditched Rachel and me last year. I don't want you to be hurt like that." Elle reached out and put her hand on Alyssa's arm. "I'm really glad we're friends, and I hope I didn't mess that up," she added.

Alyssa sighed softly. "You didn't mess it up. You *messed* up...." She laughed as Elle's eyebrows rose in surprise. "But you didn't mess up our friendship. Friends are allowed to make mistakes."

Chapter 11

When Alyssa's alarm went off bright and early the next morning, she groaned. Dasher stood up, stretched, and then lay back down. She looked at Alyssa as if to say, "It's not time to get up yet."

Alyssa smiled and gave Dasher a quick kiss on the head. "You stay in bed if you want to," she told the cat. "I have to get up and work on my knitting."

Alyssa had spent most of the rest of the afternoon and evening working on her holiday-wish essay. It was all finished now, but she was glad she had a few days to let it sit and then edit it before it was due on Friday. After she'd finished her essay, her mom and brother had convinced her to spend the rest of the night watching Christmas movies with them.

"Your knitting can wait," Cody had told her. "This is about quality time—not knitting time. Christmas only comes once a year!"

Alyssa had relented. The truth was, it didn't take much convincing. After the rough morning she'd had with her friends, an evening spent hanging out with her mom and brother was just what she needed. She'd told them about what had happened. Her mom had hugged her and told her she was proud for telling Elle and Rachel how she felt, even if it meant disagreeing with them.

Later, Alyssa had told Cody what Rachel had said about Becca only wanting to be friends with her because of the knitting. Cody's face had scrunched up in confusion. "No offense, Alyssa," he'd said, "but knitting is not some impossible-to-learn skill. Becca can learn how to knit from a book or the internet. Why would she use you for that?"

Alyssa had laughed. "I'm only slightly offended," she'd replied. "But do you really think Becca really likes me and wants to be my friend?"

"Yes, I think she does," Cody had said. "But you know the best way to find out? Talk to her about it!"

When did Cody get so good at giving advice? Alyssa wondered now as she padded down the stairs with her knitting basket. She was about two-thirds of the way done with the red ombré scarf. She'd abandoned the idea of adding embroidered details when she was finished. There simply wasn't enough time. It was a shame she hadn't gotten to see Becca's work yesterday, she thought as she settled on the couch, the Christmas tree in her field of vision. But she was hopeful that Becca really was some sort of knitting prodigy and had somehow completed four scarves already. *I'll be lucky if I finish two scarves by the deadline.*

Before long, it was time to get ready for school. Alyssa's mom had the week off from work and was going to call the vet first thing that morning to see about bringing Dasher in for her checkup. Every time Alyssa thought about it, she got nervous wondering if Dasher belonged to another family who was looking for her. But then she would remind herself of what her friends had all told her: Dasher belonged with *her*.

❄ ❄ ❄

Alyssa was eager to talk to Becca at school but didn't have a chance to see her until the very end of the day. She had looked for her at lunch, but the soccer table was empty. Then she remembered that Cody had mentioned something about a soccer team pizza party during lunchtime.

She was happy to see Becca waiting by her locker at the end of the day.

"Hey, Becca," Alyssa said, waving. "I was looking for you all day!"

A relieved grin lit up Becca's face. "Really? You have no idea how glad I am to hear that. Alyssa, I feel awful about yesterday. I am so sorry I lied to you and messed everything up."

"You didn't mess everything up," Alyssa replied. She remembered saying almost the exact same thing to Elle the previous day. *It really is crazy how similar they are*, she thought. But then she forced the thought from her head. There was no sense in dwelling on what good friends she thought Rachel, Elle, and Becca *should* be.

Becca asked if they could talk and Alyssa agreed. They decided to take the bus back to Alyssa's house together.

Once they were settled in their seats at the back of the bus, where they could have some privacy, Becca took a deep breath. "I only lied to you because I thought Elle and Rachel wouldn't want me at the sleepover. I...I was a pretty bad friend to them last year, and I don't blame them if they don't like me."

Alyssa looked out the window to gather her thoughts, as she wanted to choose her words carefully. She wanted to tell Becca that she knew otherwise—that Elle and Rachel did still care about her and did still want to be her friend—but she had also promised herself she wasn't going to get involved anymore. "I understand why you lied," she said finally. "For the record, I don't think Elle and Rachel dislike you, but I also don't think I should get in the middle of things anymore." She took a deep breath and continued. "All three of you are my friends and really important to me, and I don't want to get caught up in everything."

"I get it!" Becca nodded. "I promise I won't put you in the middle. I'm sorry about what happened at your house, and I'm just glad you're my friend."

Here goes nothing, Alyssa thought as Cody's words echoed in her head. "Actually, Becca, can I ask you something?" When Becca nodded, Alyssa continued. She nervously picked at a hole in the seat of the bus. "Why do you want to be my friend?"

Becca looked confused for a moment. "Because you're great," she said, raising her eyebrows in emphasis. "You're funny and cool and nice, and—"

"Okay, I get it," Alyssa said, laughing. "You don't have to tell me how amazing I am! I just wanted to make sure that it's not..." She hesitated. "It's not just because you wanted to learn to knit, right?"

Becca burst out laughing. "Of course not! Alyssa, knitting is not that big of a deal to me!"

"Ouch," Alyssa teased.

"You know what I mean!" Becca exclaimed. "I mean, I like knitting, but I like it because you get so excited about it. Beyond that, I can take it or leave it."

Alyssa grinned as the bus pulled up to her stop. The girls exited the bus together, and Alyssa asked Becca if she could come over. "Speaking of knitting, maybe we can have a knitting session right now?" Alyssa asked.

Becca shook her head. "I'm sorry, I can't. I have not even begun work on my holiday-wish essay, and I need to tackle that. I promised my parents no more knitting until I finished my assignment. But don't worry, I finished three more scarves this weekend, so I have seven."

"Seven?" Alyssa sputtered. "I'm just finishing up my first one!"

"Oh, really?" Becca shrugged. "But like I said, I guess I'm just fast."

"Becca, for someone who doesn't *love* knitting, you do realize that you're some kind of prodigy, right? My friend Ryder can't even knit that fast!"

Becca shrugged again. "I don't know. Maybe the stitches I'm using are more basic?"

"Still…" Alyssa shook her head in amazement. "Anyway, good luck on your essay!"

Becca gave Alyssa a quick hug. "Thanks again for being such a good friend! And I almost forgot… can you sleep over at my house on Friday night? To make up for me missing your sleepover this past weekend?"

"I'll need to check with my mom, but that should be okay," Alyssa replied. "But not to make up for missing my sleepover—I told you, I forgive you. Friends can make mistakes."

Becca grinned happily. "Got it! So this will be a knitting-slash-holiday celebration sleepover! We can watch movies, knit, eat tons of Christmas cookies…."

"Perfect—as long as you didn't bake the cookies!" Alyssa quipped.

"I deserve that." Becca laughed. "See you tomorrow!"

As Alyssa walked up to her house, she saw that her mom had put up some Christmas decorations outside. A wreath was on the front door, single white candles were in each window, and lights dangled from the bushes. Alyssa grinned happily, realizing Christmas was just around the corner and, better yet, with not one but *two* holiday sleepovers planned. It finally felt like Christmas!

Chapter 12

The next day at school flew by. During lunch, Alyssa discussed with Elle and Rachel ideas for their holiday-wish essays. Alyssa couldn't believe she was the only one who had completed hers already. But then again, she'd been really inspired!

"So what's yours about?" Elle asked for the fifth time as she peeled an orange. "Are you going to keep us in suspense or what?"

Alyssa laughed. "I will tell you, I promise! I'm still fine-tuning it. And it's kind of hard to explain."

Elle wrinkled her nose. "What did you wish for that's so complicated? World peace?"

"Nothing that complicated. Let's just say it's nothing super exciting, but it came from my heart," Alyssa said finally.

"Hmmm…" Elle said, comically stroking her chin like a cartoon villain. "I will find out. I have my ways…."

"Ignore her," Rachel whispered to Alyssa, and they both giggled. "Hey, has Dasher been to the vet yet?"

Alyssa shook her head. "She's actually going this afternoon. I'll find out after school how it went." She exhaled nervously.

"It's going to be fine," Elle said encouragingly. "That cat *chose* you. I'm positive you will get to keep her."

"I sure hope so." Alyssa bit her lip. She knew there was no use in dwelling on what *might* happen, but even still she couldn't help but worry. She'd become so attached to Dasher, she couldn't imagine having to give her up.

"How's the knitting coming along?" Rachel asked.

Alyssa appreciated the change of subject, even if the thought of knitting was stressful for her, too, though in a different way. "Very slowly. I finished the first scarf—the red ombré one—last night. Dasher fell asleep on it while I was working on it!" She took a sip of her chocolate milk. "I started on the second one. It will have a chevron pattern, so it's a little more complicated but I think it will be really pretty when it's done. I FaceTimed with Ryder last night, and he helped me figure out the pattern."

"Is Becca still helping you?"

Alyssa swallowed, unsure of how to respond. She didn't want to talk too much about Becca, but since Elle had asked she figured it was okay to answer. "Yeah, she is. She's been doing a lot. But she had to take a break to work on her essay."

Alyssa wasn't sure if she imagined it or not, but she felt like an awkward silence fell over the table. Finally, Elle broke the silence. "So, yeah, speaking of our holiday essays, let's go back to that. What on earth am I wishing for?"

❄ ❄ ❄

Alyssa practically ran home from the bus stop after school. She couldn't wait to hear how Dasher had made out at the vet.

"Mom, I'm home!" she called as she rushed into the kitchen. She saw Dasher's food bowl on the mat in the corner of the room and figured that was a good sign. "Mom? How did it go?"

"I'm in the den," Mrs. Sing replied.

Alyssa scooped up Dasher, who had ambled into the kitchen at the sound of Alyssa's voice, and gave her a kiss on her head. "What did the vet say?" she asked as she walked into the den. She placed Dasher on the ground. "I wonder if we've been overfeeding her...." she murmured. "Did the vet think she was too fat?"

"About that..." Mrs. Sing patted the couch cushion next to her. "Sit, Alyssa. I have some news."

Alyssa felt a wave of panic but then realized her mom didn't look upset. She was smiling...sort of. "What? Is Dasher okay?" she wailed. "Do we have to give her back to someone? Tell me!"

"One question at a time," Mrs. Sing said. "First and foremost—she is fine. She's a healthy young cat. The vet thinks she's about three years old." Alyssa breathed a sigh of relief. "However, the vet had a pretty big surprise for us...." Her mom paused dramatically. "Dasher is pregnant! The vet thinks she's due to have her kittens in a week or two, though it can be hard to pinpoint an exact date."

"Pregnant?" Alyssa cried. "I can't believe it!"

"There's more," her mom continued. "She did have a microchip. They pulled up the information from the database for the owners she was registered to and tried contacting them, but the phone number was no longer in service."

"So that means she's ours!" Alyssa cheered.

"We'll see, sweetie," her mom said, placing her hand on Alyssa's arm. "They also have an email address and were going to reach out via email to see if the owners can be found. They have to try, Alyssa," she added when Alyssa began to protest. "I don't want to give you false hope, but the doctor did say that a lot of the time in these situations, the emails go unanswered. And there were no reports at the Palm Meadows animal shelter that she was missing, so it may be that her owners were ready to give her up."

"Mom, this is great news," Alyssa cried. She felt like her head was spinning. "We have so much to fig-ure out about the kittens! Did you find out what we need to do? We can still keep her, right?" Alyssa had so many questions. "I know kittens are a big responsibility, but I already know a little bit about the local animal shelter and I think they can help us out if we can't find homes for all her kittens, but I'm sure we can. I bet my friends would take some, and maybe Mrs. Amir would want one...."

Mrs. Sing laughed. "Yes, I got some pamphlets with all the information. And the vet was sure we have at least another week or two so we can bring her back right before Christmas for another checkup to see how she's coming along. That gives us some time to prepare for the kittens."

Alyssa felt a huge rush of love for her mom. *She's going to let me keep her!*

"Mom, I know this is going to be a lot of work, and more than you signed up for when you let me get a cat. I *promise* you, I will take such good care of Dasher and her kittens and I will find a great home for every single one of them!"

"I know you will, sweetie," her mom said. She smiled ruefully. "It's definitely not what I expected when we took her in, but if she's going to be our cat, we have to make sure to do right by her. She's our family now." She kissed Alyssa's head as she stood up. "It looks like this Christmas is going to be one to remember for sure!"

❄ ❄ ❄

Later that evening, Alyssa, Cody, and Mrs. Sing sat around the kitchen table constructing a gingerbread house. This was one of Alyssa's favorite Christmas traditions, and with everything going on this year, she had almost forgotten all about it! Luckily, her mom hadn't forgotten and brought home a gingerbread house kit for them to use. Cody was an expert at applying the "glue," which was really icing, to hold the pieces together.

"I'm thinking a border of cinnamon candies along the edges of the roof," she murmured as she carefully applied the last bit of icing. "What do you think, Cody?"

"That works," he agreed. "I'm going to see if I can make some Christmas lights using the licorice strings and fruit DOTS."

"Ooh, good idea!"

As they worked, Mrs. Sing asked Alyssa if she had finished her holiday-wish essay. Alyssa said that she had, and Mrs. Sing asked her if she could tell them her wish.

"I wrote about wanting our first Christmas in Florida to be really special," Alyssa explained. "I talked about how, just a couple of weeks ago, I didn't feel comfortable here yet because I didn't really have any friends and I wasn't used to the weather being so warm for Christmas and how strange it all seemed. How homesick I was." She paused to count out another row of cinnamon candies. "But so much happened in such a short time—it really started to feel like Christmas, and I made friends, and found Dasher...."

Alyssa looked up at her mother and brother. "I said in my essay that my wish had already come true and how grateful I am for everything. This is our home, and I'm glad we're here." She felt her cheeks burn a little as she talked about it, wondering if it sounded dumb. "It's not the most exciting essay in the world, but it came from my heart and that's what Mrs. Ramirez wanted, so I'm pretty happy with how it turned out."

"Alyssa, honey, that sounds wonderful," her mom

said, a smile lighting up her face. "I am glad you're so happy. You deserve it!"

"Yeah." Cody nodded. "That actually sounds like a really good essay."

"Aww, Cody, look at you being all sweet!" Alyssa teased, tossing a cinnamon candy at her brother.

Cody caught the candy in his mouth. "Not really," he replied. "You didn't let me finish. I was just about to say that it's a Christmas miracle you made friends so quickly!"

"Ha-ha," Alyssa said, pretending to be upset. But she knew her brother was only joking. She also knew how lucky she was to have him for a brother.

Chapter 13

The rest of the week flew by for Alyssa in a blur of knitting, researching how to care for kittens, and putting the finishing touches on her holiday-wish essay. When Alyssa finally handed the essay in on Friday morning, she did so with a lot of pride. She had lingered behind all the other kids, wanting to be the last one to hand in her essay so she could say something to her teacher.

"Thank you, Alyssa," Mrs. Ramirez said as she accepted the paper from Alyssa. "I hope you have a wonderful holiday."

"Thanks, Mrs. Ramirez," Alyssa replied. "I really

enjoyed writing my essay...." She looked at the ground. She wasn't used to talking to her teachers unless she was called on, but she wanted Mrs. Ramirez to know how much she had enjoyed the assignment. "It was nice to stop and think about what's really important during the holidays. It helped make Christmas extra special for me. I hope you like my essay."

Mrs. Ramirez beamed. "I'm sure I will love it, Alyssa. And thank you for letting me know you enjoyed the assignment. That's always wonderful to hear."

❋ ❋ ❋

I can't believe it's finally holiday break! Alyssa thought later that day as she walked home from the bus stop. Given the situation with Dasher, Becca had agreed to move their sleepover to Alyssa's house that night so Alyssa wouldn't have to be away from her pregnant cat for the whole night, especially since she was having a sleepover at Elle's the following evening. "No problem at all," Becca had said when Alyssa had asked her about it.

"Just remember to bring your knitting with you

so I can finally see all these scarves you've made!" Alyssa reminded her.

Alyssa was so excited about being off from school and Christmas being just around the corner that when she walked into her house it took her a moment to register that her mom looked very, very upset.

"Mom, what's wrong?" Alyssa asked.

"Sit down, sweetie," Mrs. Sing said, motioning to a kitchen chair.

"Is it Dasher?"

Mrs. Sing nodded. "She's okay, Alyssa—nothing bad has happened to her. But her owners showed up. They got the email from the vet and drove all the way to the vet's office today to claim Dasher. They had moved out of Palm Meadows about six months ago, and Dasher got loose during their move. They had reported her missing, but it somehow never went into the database at the animal shelter. They thought they had lost her forever."

"I—I don't understand," Alyssa said, looking around the kitchen and noticing Dasher's food bowl was gone. "Where is she?"

"Honey, the vet called this morning not long after you left for school and told me her owners had shown up. I had to bring her to give her back."

"She's gone?" Alyssa cried. "And I didn't even get to say goodbye?"

Mrs. Sing's eyes filled with tears as Alyssa's face crumbled. "I know, Alyssa. I'm so sorry. I asked them if they could wait and let you say goodbye, but they had driven a few hours to get here and they just really wanted to take her home. For what it's worth, they were really nice people and they seemed so happy to be reunited with her. I gave them my phone number and asked if we could keep in touch."

"I can't believe she's gone," Alyssa said. She fell into her mom's arms and sobbed like her heart was breaking. And it really felt to her like it was.

❄ ❄ ❄

A little while later, Mrs. Sing knocked on Alyssa's door. She'd gone to lie down after crying her eyes out about Dasher.

"Alyssa, Elle is on the phone. Are you up to speaking with her?"

"Yeah," Alyssa replied, getting out of bed and taking the phone from her mom.

"Alyssa, change of plans!" Elle was saying as Alyssa put the phone to her ear. "Rachel's parents forgot that our sleepover was tomorrow night and invited her cousins over. She wouldn't be able to make it tomorrow night, so we have to switch our sleepover to tonight. Can you be here in an hour?"

"Wait, what?" Alyssa felt like her head was still fuzzy from all the crying. "Elle, I can't tonight. I... I..." Alyssa was about to tell her about Dasher but couldn't bring herself to. She was afraid she'd start crying again.

"Why can't you?" Elle demanded. "What's wrong? Please come—you *have* to come! Do you need me to explain to your mom—"

"No, it's not that," Alyssa said. "I already made plans with Becca. She's coming over tonight."

Elle was silent on the other end of the phone, and Alyssa knew she'd upset her. "I'm sorry, Elle, but I can't change my plans."

"Why not?" Elle asked. "I mean, we had this

sleepover planned since last week, and you know how important it is to us. We really want you here, Alyssa. Please?"

"I'm sorry, I can't," Alyssa repeated.

"Fine. I see," Elle said.

"Please don't be mad," Alyssa added, taking a shaky breath. "It's been a really bad day for me, and—"

"And you'd rather be cheered up by Becca than Rachel and me. I get it."

"No, that's not what I meant!" Alyssa exclaimed.

"Look, Alyssa, I have to go. I'll talk to you later, okay?" Elle's voice cracked a little, and Alyssa could hear how upset she was. "Have fun tonight with Becca."

With that, Elle hung up the phone, and Alyssa started to cry all over again.

❄ ❄ ❄

When Alyssa's mom poked her head in Alyssa's room a little while later and saw Alyssa crying on her bed, she sat down next to her and rubbed her back.

Alyssa rolled over to face her mom and tried to explain her argument with Elle, but it didn't even make sense to her. "How can she expect me to cancel my plans with Becca just because their plans changed? Can you believe she's mad at me now?" Alyssa asked.

Her mom tucked a strand of hair behind Alyssa's ear. "I bet she's not really angry, Alyssa. You didn't do anything wrong, and deep down, Elle knows that."

Alyssa sniffled. "I know what a big deal this sleepover was to her and Rachel, and I really wanted to go. This is the sleepover that Becca canceled on them last year at the last minute, so I know how sensitive they are about it. I maybe would have asked Becca to switch nights, but I was just so upset about everything with Dasher that I didn't even think of it at the time." She sat up in bed. "Mom, this *is* my fault. Why didn't I think of that?"

"You are not blaming yourself for this, Alyssa," Mrs. Sing said firmly. Her voice softened as she squeezed Alyssa's hand. "Like we talked about last weekend, you can't get stuck in the middle of whatever is going on between these girls. And later, after you feel better, I hope you'll talk to Elle about all of this and let her know she has to choose her words more carefully in the future. Don't be afraid to tell her how you feel, sweetie."

Alyssa nodded. She knew her mom was right, but it wasn't that easy. She didn't want to lose Elle's friendship.

"Becca is supposed to arrive soon. Are you up for having her over tonight? It might help to have a friend to lean on, sweetie, but if you're not up to it, I can let Becca know. Plus, Cody and I will be here for you."

Alyssa wiped her eyes. "I'm going to think about it. I'll let you know, okay?"

As Mrs. Sing left her room, Alyssa walked over to the mirror that was above her dresser. She almost didn't recognize herself. Her eyes were red and puffy, and her face was all flushed from crying. Her eyes wandered over to her desk, where she saw the extra printout of her holiday-wish essay. Picking it up, she scanned the page and felt her eyes fill up with tears again.

So, in all these ways, I feel that my holiday wish has already come true. My new house in Florida really feels like a home for the holidays because of all the wonderful memories we have made here. I've made three amazing new friends, and I've even gotten the cat I always wanted. This is shaping up to be the perfect Christmas, even better than anything I could have wished for, and I am so grateful!

Alyssa couldn't believe that just twenty-four hours ago those words had been true. And now she felt so far away from almost everything she had written.

Just then, Alyssa heard a gentle knock at her door.

"Hey, can I come in?" Becca asked.

Alyssa nodded.

"Your mom told me what happened with Dasher. I am so, so sorry." Becca's face was filled with concern. "What can I do, Alyssa?"

Alyssa sighed and sat on the bed, her essay still in her hand. "I don't know what anyone can do," she replied. She folded her essay in half and tossed it on her nightstand. "I don't think I will be very good company tonight, Becca. Would you mind if we rescheduled?"

"Of course not," Becca said, sitting down on the bed next to Alyssa. "Do you want me to tell your mom to call Rachel and Elle and let them know about Dasher so you don't have to? I'm sure they would want to know."

"That's really sweet," Alyssa replied. "But they're mad at me. Well, Elle is anyway." She told Becca about her phone call with Elle.

"That's terrible," Becca cried. "But, Alyssa, I know Elle didn't mean it. She just has a bit of a temper and says things she doesn't mean. That's one of the reasons I have been so scared to try to make up with her!" Becca patted Alyssa's arm. "But I'm sure that if she knew about Dasher she'd feel absolutely terrible...."

Alyssa shook her head. "No, I don't want her to feel terrible. I just...I just don't want to think about it right now. I'm too upset about Dasher. Is that okay with you?"

"Of course," Becca repeated. She gave Alyssa a gentle hug. "Call me later if you need to talk, okay?"

Alyssa said goodbye to her friend and lay back down on her bed. She knew that lying around wallowing wasn't going to help matters, but right now that was all she really felt like doing.

Chapter 14

Less than an hour later, Alyssa was in the kitchen with Cody, helping their mom prepare dinner. They were making homemade pizza.

"Allow me," Cody said, gently elbowing Alyssa out of the way. He rearranged the pieces of green pepper on top of the pizza so they resembled a Christmas tree.

"Voilà," he said.

Alyssa smiled a little. She appreciated that her brother was trying to cheer her up.

"Is someone at the door?" Mrs. Sing said from

the counter where she was cleaning mushrooms. "Will one of you kids go get that?"

Alyssa opened the front door and was surprised to see Elle standing there.

"I heard what happened to Dasher," Elle explained. Her next words came out in a rush, classic Elle style. "I am so, so *sorry*. And I am so sorry I was so rude on the phone before. I had no idea about Dasher obviously, but still, I shouldn't have asked you to cancel your plans. I was just hurt, but I shouldn't have taken it out on you. Can you forgive me?"

Alyssa leaned against the doorframe and took a deep breath. *Mom was right. I need to tell her how I feel.* "I can forgive you, Elle, but this is the second time in a week that you got really upset with me and said something unfair. It's nice that you apologized after, but if we're going to be friends, I really need for you to not do that to me. When we don't agree on stuff, I need to be able to say something without you getting mad at me."

I can't believe I just said that, Alyssa thought. *But it felt good. It needed to be said.*

Elle nodded and looked down at her shoes. "You

are absolutely right, Alyssa," she added quickly. "I know I need to slow down and calm down, especially when it comes to you. In fact, that's what I wrote my holiday-wish essay about...." She looked up, and Alyssa saw that her friend was blushing. "I wished I could learn to not fly off the handle when I get upset. I said I was afraid I was going to lose a really good friend over it. But please don't tell anyone that. It's kind of majorly embarrassing."

Alyssa smiled and moved away from the door, gesturing for Elle to come in. "That sounds like an awesome essay," she replied. It felt good to know she was so important to Elle that she had written her holiday-wish essay about being a better friend to her. She grinned a genuine grin for the first time since hearing the news about Dasher. "Do you want to come in? We're making pizza."

"OMG, I almost forgot!" Elle exclaimed. "Can you come over? I—" She held up a hand as a shocked look crossed Alyssa's face. "Becca is over. Actually, she's in the car, with my mom and Rachel." She moved to the side, and Alyssa noticed Elle's mom's car in the driveway with Becca and Rachel in the back seat.

They all waved to Alyssa. "Becca literally *ran* over to my house to tell us what happened, and we want you to come over so your three best friends can cheer you up. I mean, she sprinted the whole way there because she was so worried about you. So, what do you say? Can we have a holiday sleepover together? I promise we will cheer you up! Rachel and I will even learn how to knit and we can spend the whole night knitting if that's what you want to do...."

"I—I—" Alyssa didn't know *what* to say.

"They came with me just in case you said no because they are not taking no for an answer and if you won't come then we're coming in," Elle added breathlessly. "And trust me, you do not want to mess with Becca when she has her mind set on something!"

Alyssa burst out laughing. "I guess that leaves me no choice! Let me get my stuff together and ask my mom. Why don't you guys all come inside while I'm packing?"

❄ ❄ ❄

A few hours later, just before nine o'clock, Alyssa, Elle, Rachel, and Becca were arranging their sleeping bags on the floor of Elle's rec room. Her house had a finished basement with the coolest rec room Alyssa had ever seen. There was a huge TV, an air hockey table, beanbag chairs, and even a second Christmas tree. The girls had stuffed themselves on Christmas cookies—that Becca had been banned from participating in the baking of—and were settling down to knit.

Alyssa pulled out the red ombré scarf from her bag just as Becca was reaching into her backpack for her completed scarves. "This is the one I finished. I don't expect you guys to do anything this fancy initially, but..."

When Becca saw Alyssa's scarf, she burst out laughing.

"What?" Alyssa exclaimed, feeling her cheeks burn. "Is something wrong with my scarf?"

"No, it's gorgeous," Becca replied between giggles. "It's just—huge!"

"What?" Alyssa was confused. "It's standard size."

"No, look," Becca said, laughing even harder as she pulled a teeny, tiny little knit scarf out to show

Alyssa. As Becca held up her tiny little scarf, Rachel and Elle burst into giggles, too.

"That's like two inches long and a quarter of an inch thick!" Alyssa cried.

"Yes, the perfect size for the dolls my aunt sells in her doll store," Becca said. "Wait, did you think my aunt's store was a boutique for people? That I was asking you to make fifteen *people* scarves?"

"Alyssa, Becca's aunt's store is that big doll store on Ocean Drive," Rachel added. She was laughing so hard she was practically gasping for air. Elle was doubled over.

"I can't believe it," Alyssa replied. "How did I not know that? Did you tell me?"

"I'm sure I did," Becca said. "Didn't I? Did I not tell you her store was a doll store? I know I told you about the little umbrellas she sold last year, right?" She pulled out all the tiny little scarves she'd knit and spread them on the floor. "Now we know how I made so many scarves and you only made one."

The girls were all laughing so hard that when Elle's mom appeared in the room a moment later

Alyssa assumed it was to ask them to keep it down. But instead she extended the phone to Alyssa. "It's your mom, sweetie. It's not an emergency, but she has to tell you something."

Alyssa accepted the phone and spoke quietly to her mom. Her friends could hear her excitedly saying things like "That's amazing!" and "How many?" and "How long?" so they knew it was good news.

When Alyssa sat back down on her sleeping bag, her face was shining with excitement. "Dasher had her kittens already!" she exclaimed. "She had five, and they are all doing well. Her owners called my mom to tell her. And the best part is…they want me to come over when the kittens are a little older so I can choose one to keep!"

"Aw, Alyssa, that's wonderful!" Rachel exclaimed.

"Maybe it's time for me to get my next cat, too!" Becca said.

"You totally should—but know that the cat will like me better!" Elle joked.

Alyssa laughed along with her friends. *I can't believe Dasher had her kittens already*, she thought. *It kind of feels like this was meant to be. I think Dasher will be happy knowing one of her babies will be coming to live with me. And I'm happy for Dasher that she's back home in time for Christmas.*

"This might be a good time to give you your Christmas gift," Becca said suddenly. She reached into her backpack and pulled out a simple knitted blanket in shades of pink, purple, and yellow. "I made this for you, for Dasher," she said shyly. "I know you can make one that's a thousand times better, but I wanted to make you something to say thank you for being such a good friend. Now you can use it for your new kitty."

Alyssa didn't know what to say. Before she could respond, Elle cleared her throat and handed Alyssa a gift bag that had been sitting on the coffee table. "And this is from Rachel and me. It's just not homemade because, well, we are not talented." She giggled.

Alyssa opened the bag and saw that it was filled with cat toys. Stuffed mice, little balls, crinkly fish... it looked like they had bought out the cat toy section of the pet store.

"You guys, this is so sweet," she said happily. "I

don't have anything for any of you, though. Maybe you can all share this ombré scarf?"

Elle, Rachel, and Becca burst out laughing

"Are you kidding?" Elle said finally. Rachel and Becca joined her in a group hug with Alyssa. "You've given us the best gift of all—friendship."

Not finished celebrating the season yet? Here's a sneak peek at another book in the series:

Celebrate the Season

Let It Snow!

Taylor Garland

Chapter 1

Chloe Warner wriggled under her bed, sneezing as dust tickled her nose. She hadn't used her suitcase since last summer—more than five months ago—and she definitely hadn't dealt with the army of dust bunnies that had sprung up since then, either. But she didn't care about that right now. In an hour, Chloe and her dad would be hitting the road for an incredible weekend at the Lodge Resort in the Pocono Mountains. And in three days, Christmas would be here!

Chloe had been counting down to the pre-Christmas getaway ever since Dad had told her about it back in October. She'd spent hours swiping through the lodge's website on her phone, imagining what it would be like to sleep in one of the rustic log cabins or ski down a snowy slope. She'd picked out the perfect dress (and the perfect accessories) for the big party on Christmas Eve Eve. The one part of the trip that Chloe wasn't able to prepare for was what it would be like to meet Dad's girlfriend, Jessica, and Jessica's daughter, Sandy, for the very first time.

Dad had told Chloe all about Jessica—that's how Chloe knew how important Jessica was to him—but it was still hard to imagine what she'd be like in person. And it was even harder to imagine what Sandy would be like, probably because Dad had never met Sandy, so there wasn't much he could tell her. Would they like the same music? Share the same hobbies? Become besties? Or would they have nothing in common at all?

Soon Chloe wouldn't have to wonder anymore.

Soon she would know!

Jeans, snow pants, shirts, sweaters—Chloe tossed

them all into her suitcase. She was a little more careful with her special dress for the party. It was made of cranberry-colored lace, with a matching slip in exactly the same color. Chloe carefully folded it and placed it right on top.

Chloe glanced over at the bed, where her dog, a cuddly white terrier named Charlie, watched her with bright, curious eyes.

"What do you think, Charlie?" Chloe asked as she held up two different shoes. "Black velvet shoes or sparkly silver ones?"

"Woof!" Charlie barked.

"I agree," Chloe said with a giggle. "Sparkly silver all the way!"

She sat on the edge of her bed and checked the list on her phone. She'd packed just about everything—her clothes, her shoes, her accessories, her snow gear. Her toiletries bag was tucked into a side pocket. But Chloe still couldn't shake the feeling that she'd forgotten something.

"What is it, Charlie?" she asked, scratching her pup behind his ears. "What did I forget?"

Suddenly, a knowing smile crossed Chloe's face. "Of course," she whispered. Chloe leaned across the bed for a framed photo on her bedside table. She couldn't leave her mom behind.

Chloe nestled the photo in the lacy folds of her party dress. Her mother had died a long time ago—Chloe had only a few vivid memories of her; the rest had grown hazy over the years—but before she fell asleep every night she still liked to look at the beautiful photo of her mother.

Chloe zipped her suitcase closed and whistled to Charlie. "Come on, buddy!" she called.

Thunk-thunk-thunk-thunk. The suitcase thudded so loudly as Chloe dragged it down the stairs that Dad poked his head out of his room to see what was making all the noise. "Hey! I would've carried your suitcase downstairs!" he called out.

"No worries! I've got it!" Chloe replied. Once she reached the first floor, she wheeled the suitcase over to the front door, where she'd already left her backpack and a duffel bag packed with Charlie's food, leash, and dishes. She was happy Dad had managed to find a hotel that allowed Charlie to stay with them. The next few minutes passed by in a blur as Dad and Chloe loaded up the car. Then Chloe settled Charlie into his special dog bed in the back seat before she climbed in and fastened her seat belt. It was almost time to go!

"Ready?" Dad asked.

"Ready!" she replied.

"Then let's hit the road!" Dad announced as he started down the driveway. Chloe reached for her backpack to check the inside pocket one more time. She already knew that she'd packed Charlie's medicine—in fact, it was the very first thing she had packed—but she wanted to be certain before they were all the way in the mountains.

"Got everything?" Dad asked with a quick sideways glance at Chloe.

"Yes," she replied. "At least, I think so. And whatever I forgot, I'll just have to do without."

Dad chuckled. "We're spending the weekend at a three-star resort in the Poconos, not going on a mountaineering expedition," he told her. "There will be plenty of stores and shops if there's anything you need."

"Thanks, Dad—I know," Chloe said. "I just want everything to be perfect!"

Chloe inhaled deeply, breathing in the scent of the miniature pine tree that she and Dad had bought as a surprise for Jessica and Sandy. The sharp, piney smell filled the car and made it feel even more like Christmastime.

"Can't believe it's finally here," Dad said, breaking the silence. "Are you excited?"

"Are you kidding?" Chloe laughed. "I've been thinking about this trip nonstop! It's going to be incredible! Do you think Sandy and Jessica will get there before we do?"

"It depends on when they leave," Dad said. "Apparently, Sandy tends to sleep in. But Jessica said she'd do her best to get them on the road by ten o'clock."

"There's no way I could've slept late today," Chloe said. "I could barely sleep last night, either."

"Same here," Dad replied. "I'm so glad that you'll finally be able to meet Jessica. She's...she's really special."

Chloe glanced at Dad out of the corner of her eye, but he was focused on the road ahead. There was something about his voice that filled her with quivery excitement. It gave her the courage to ask the question that had been on her mind for months.

"Dad?" she began. "Are you going to ask Jessica to marry you?"

"Marry me?" Dad repeated. He started to laugh— a laugh that was both surprised and kind. "I don't know, Chloe. Marriage is a big commitment...one that should last a lifetime. We're not quite there yet. But Jessica means a lot to me, which is why I'm so excited for you two to meet. It's way past time for the most important ladies in my life to finally know each other."

"Got it," Chloe said. "I was just thinking...if you marry Jessica...then Sandy would be, like, my sister. Stepsister—whatever."

"That would be a big change, wouldn't it?" Dad asked.

"The sister I've always wanted!" Chloe joked. At least, she tried to make a joke. But in her heart, she'd always longed for a sibling. A sister—a sister her own age—would be like a dream come true.

Don't get carried away, Chloe told herself. After all, she'd never even met Sandy before.

But there was no harm in hoping—right?

❄ ❄ ❄

Two hours later, Dad and Chloe finally arrived at the lodge. The lobby had been so extensively decorated—there were swooping pine garlands, strands of twinkling lights, and enormous Christmas trees everywhere Chloe looked—that she didn't even mind the wait while Dad checked in.

"All set!" Dad finally announced. He handed Chloe her own key. "Keep this in a safe place, okay? We'll be staying in Sugar Plum Cottage."

"Sugar Plum Cottage?" Chloe repeated with a grin.

Dad grinned back. "They rename all the cottages for December," he explained. "Jessica and Sandy are in Mistletoe Cottage—which is just a short walk from ours."

Chloe's heart started to beat a little faster. "Do you mean—are they here?" she asked.

"They sure are. Jessica texted me twenty minutes

ago," Dad told her. "Let's get settled into our cottage and then we can—"

"Let's go over there right now!" Chloe said in excitement.

Dad chuckled. "All right, all right. But let's at least bring our luggage inside first," he said. "And maybe we should wait a little while to bring them the Christmas tree."

Chloe giggled. "It would probably look pretty weird if we just showed up with a tree without any warning," she replied.

Together, Dad and Chloe unloaded the car and took a quick tour of Sugar Plum Cottage. It was filled with rustic decorations—patchwork quilts, woven baskets, lamps in the shape of lanterns, and a weathered pine box filled with chopped-up wood by the fireplace.

"Hey, we have three bedrooms," Chloe said. "Does that mean Charlie gets his own room?"

"If he wants it," Dad said. "But I have a feeling he'll be sticking close to you, like always."

"Which room is mine?" she asked.

"Whichever one you want," Dad told her.

Chloe finally decided on the bedroom with a window seat that offered an amazing view of the snow-covered mountains. She didn't want to waste time unpacking, but there was one important thing Chloe wanted to do before she, Dad, and Charlie set off for Mistletoe Cottage. She unzipped her suitcase and pulled out Mom's photo. Once the photo was sitting on her bedside table, Chloe almost felt like she was at home. She adjusted the frame so that she could see Mom's loving smile better.

"Here goes," Chloe whispered to the photo. "Wish me luck!"

Not finished celebrating the season yet? Check out these other feel-good books in the series: